Of Myths and Mothers

An anthology of stories

By Kenzie Millar, Gaynor Jones, Sascha Akhtar,
Clayton Lister and Helen Nathaniel-Fulton

First published 25th of March 2022 by Fly on the Wall Press
Published in the UK by
Fly on the Wall Press
56 High Lea Rd
New Mills
Derbyshire
SK22 3DP

www.flyonthewallpress.co.uk

ISBN Print: 978-1-913211-78-3
EBook: 978-1-913211-79-0
Copyright remains with individual authors © 2022

The right of Kenzie Millar, Gaynor Jones, Sascha Akhtar,
Clayton Lister and Helen Nathaniel-Fulton to be indetified as the
authors of their individual works, and Isabelle Kenyon as the editor
of this work has been asserted in accordance with the Copyright,
Designs and Patents Act 1988.

Typesetting by Isabelle Kenyon.
Cover illustration by Kayla Jenkins.

Praise for Of Myths and Mothers:

"Given that two of my biggest blindspots are historical fiction and epistolary fiction and I still loved her story, I must put that down to Kenzie Millar's silky prose and the thrilling wonders she teases out of the depths."

- Nicholas Royle, Writer, Editor and Judge of the Manchester Fiction Prize

"Jones has created an unsettling, near-the-bone world in May We Know Them, with taut, vivid prose that grips the reader. A triumph of short fiction; this is the type of piece that the genre was made for."

- Catherine Menon, Author of Fragile Monsters;

"Helen Nathaniel-Fulton's electric combination of the visceral and compassionate invites the reader into her memories of post-war Germany where, as a student worker. she competes with immigrants for a range of appallingly brutal and mind-numbing jobs. She witnesses overt racism towards and among the immigrants, and must endure sexism towards herself. The deceptively calm tone draws the reader in, as though these stories are being related over a cup of coffee - but watch out for those narrative swerves! It's a riveting read and belongs on your bedside table."

- Sandra Hunter, Author of Losing Touch

"Once again, Lister brings us a tale of an imperfect family, cracked but not shattered. In this tale, we sit beside the teller, in front of a roaring fire; we find ourselves within a noisy, chaotic, remote (and maybe witchy) Yorkshire farmstead, filled with the drama of everyday life."

— Rose Drew, Poet and Anthropologist, and Editor at Stairwell Books, York.

Contents:

May We Know Them
Gaynor Jones

Moses

They find it at the end of their fishing weekend. A small basket floating in the river near their camp. They slip on stones, hands out for balance, pull it toward them with the aid of fallen branches and when that doesn't work, their rods.

The basket is not made of reeds, but worn, plastic strips that might once have been part of a child's toy shopping basket. Still, Helen and Juliana are more than familiar with the Bible, and so the name Moses comes to each of them at the same time.

They debate whether to send it to carry on down the river, to perhaps say a prayer over it, release it back into the water, watch it disappear from their lives. This is all communicated wordlessly in the raising of Helen's eyebrow, beneath her bluntly cut fringe. In the flush of colour in Juliana's hollow cheeks. In the air that hangs stagnant between them. They stand, ankle deep, the warm water seeping into their boots until Helen offers her hand to Juliana. They move together, carry the basket and the thing within it to the riverbank and place it on the dry earth, steady and sure. They look at it resting on the ground where the guts of the trout they caught earlier lie browning in the afternoon heat and form a heart shape above its head.

Juliana

The small courtyard hummed with the buzz of pollen-drunk bees weaving in and out of foxglove bells. Juliana kicked at a wrangle of tall daisies creeping out from under the bench, her canvas sneakers tinged green beneath her knee-high socks. Her mother looked over at the thick pad of cotton Juliana held to her upper arm and said,

"They might as well have robots doing it."

Juliana shrugged, then winced.

"Maybe they will."

But her mother was wrong. Yes, it had been quick, and yes, Juliana had been one of many young girls lined up, and yes it had been efficient. But the woman herself had been kind, attentive. She'd smiled at Juliana, shown her where the apple juice and plain biscuits were for after, lifted her gently by the elbow as she moved her from the chair to the cubicle. Juliana could still feel the place under the injection site where the woman's fingers had pressed softly against her flesh. She smoothed her fingers over it and felt her breath quicken at the memory.

Juliana's mother fussed with the papers on her lap, then looked up at the sky, a stark white matted with thick clouds that threatened another flood, the third in as many weeks. Juliana moved closer to her mother on the bench, who in turn pressed her body back. Juliana pulled the pad away from her arm altogether and held it in her lap. Just a pinprick of colour, a much brighter red than the dull streak she had seen on the paper after wiping herself that morning. The arm wasn't sore, not exactly. It was more of a throbbing sensation, akin to a pulse.

She knew that some girls preferred to wait a few days, so the pain of the injection didn't add to the pain low down, in that strange and secret place above their thighs, but Juliana's mother had wanted it all done quickly.

Juliana had heard that some families held parties in those few short days, with paper streamers and lemonade and sometimes even a cake. But Juliana agreed with her mother — what was there to celebrate? Sometimes, girls at school held their own muted ceremonies, bundled under cool willow dens, dusty mudpies stacked on top of each other, presented with whispered laughs hiding the questions underneath, while Juliana traced shapes in the dirt.

Her mother's voice pulled her back to the courtyard.

"Your great grandfather had excellent bedside manner. He was deputy director, you know."

Juliana nodded. She knew; didn't his dusty, uniformed portrait still hang among the pictures on the stairwell? Their family. Photos of her mother, hands on her stomach, her smile beaming, and of Juliana, her chubby fists fading behind the glass.

"And your father, he could have been…"

Juliana looked up at the sky. A flash crackled between the clouds.

"We should go home, Mother."

Her mother nodded and rose from the bench. She put her arms around her daughter, careful not to rub at the spot just below her shoulder.

Moses

The basket stays on the rock as they go through their usual, well-heeled routine. They tighten the lids on their plastic bait boxes. Juliana throws a couple of maggots out to the fish still grumbling in the river, by way of thanks. Helen pulls the poles from the tent, muscles flexing, sliding and folding and bending the metal into smaller and smaller lengths, like a puzzle. They each hold two corners of the damp canvas, flap it into the breeze, pull leaves, mulch and slugs from the bottom, then pass the canvas neatly to each other, corner to corner like an old folk dance. The final fish is placed in the ice box and the ice box placed in the trunk. The blood and entrails are rinsed from the rock. They dip their hands into the water to wash away any debris, kneeling quietly next to each other: no splashing, no flicking, no teasing. Not today. They rise, the campsite blank and empty around them. Apart from the basket. It seems right to take it, to pack it up with all the other things. It seems like the right thing to do.

On the drive home, the cylinder in the centre of the dashboard flashes from green to orange. Helen taps it, as if her fingertips might replenish the power. This might be their last fishing trip for a while. The worn tires rattle on the road, but inside all is quiet. No sounds from the women in the front, or from the trunk where the basket lies, wedged in-between the fishing rods and blankets. They had drilled airholes in there to carry the worst of the smells out after one of their early, claustrophobic fishing trips when they had been testing each other out as much as the water. The trunk isn't pleasant, but it is safe. Soon, the wheels crunch along the familiar gravel path. The engine clicks off. They sit. Usually, they have a quick embrace before they go home. But tonight, they stay in their seats, belts loosely fastened round their waists. Helen looks straight ahead at the house. Juliana chews on her thumbnail.

"Shall we..?"

Helen's voice trails off, but it's enough. Juliana moves. Together, they move from car to house from house to car, return all of their known, familiar things back to the spaces waiting for them. Until there is only one thing left.

"What about..?"

Juliana looks at Helen. They stand at either end of the open trunk. The moonlight casts their shadows onto the basket. And if the thing laid inside it hadn't gurgled, just at that moment – the slurred watery noise cutting through the quiet of the night sky – perhaps it would be there still.

Helen

There was a rumour that Callie Henderson's dog somehow had care of a pile of puppies. But as Helen arrived at the Henderson's yard with her rucksack over her shoulder, it was clear that the rumour was just that. The dog slunk on the dusty floor in the sweltering heat, alone, as it always had done.

The dog was well known on the estate, because it had a curious habit: after eating any food, no matter the size of the meal, it would pace and shiver until it was given a balled-up pile of socks that Callie and her sisters had long outgrown. The dog would pine and pine until it was given the sock-ball, then it would carry it around, threads hanging from its mouth, unable to relax until it had re-buried it somewhere safe.

"My Mam said he thinks it's a baby, and the howling is 'cause he feels bad that he didn't give it no food."

Helen screwed up her face.

"Your dog is stupid. Besides, you know boys can't have babies…"

Helen's voice trailed off and they watched the small dog scratching at the ground. With the top of her arm still stinging, Helen tossed the dog a scrap of sun-hardened crust from the bread Callie's mother had left out. Even that tasteless morsel was enough to trigger the searching and howling. Helen dug up the sock-ball from its hiding place at the edge of the porch. Her nose wrinkled at the stench as she lifted it to her face. But instead of letting the poor dog take it from her hand, she began to back off, away from the porch, toward the loose-hanging gate.

"Hey!"

Callie's mother, roused by the noise, glared at Helen from the doorway, her dirty washcloth still in her hand, her steamed glasses pushed up onto the top of her head. Helen felt the twitch of the injection site in her left arm and stood firm.

"Helen Carpenter, you give that back or there'll be something coming for you!"

The dog, more confident now that the matriarch had arrived, slowed its pacing, ears cocked, legs weak. Helen stayed for a moment, watching the dog.

It had been wild and loud just a few moments earlier, now it sat. Silent. Subdued.

Helen took a sharp breath, glared once more at the stern woman before her and the pathetic creature trembling at her feet. Then she ran. She ran, the sock-ball in her hand, her arms pumping quickly, she ran even as she heard the noises from behind her – yelling, heavy footsteps, her name over and over – and soon enough she was in the woods, where the cool trees wrapped themselves around her. Coated in sweat so that her cotton dress stuck to her, she leaned against a thick trunk to catch her breath and listened to the desperate yap-yapping getting closer, closer.

She could have stopped then.

Could have turned around and said it was all a tease.

Could have given the stupid sock-ball of a baby back to the dog and taken the slap from Callie's mother.

Instead, she heaved herself up and forwards, towards the muddy stream where mosquitoes hovered and dipped and smog floated in the air, her arm pulled far back, ready to hurl the damned thing into the murky water, when she saw a figure across the way.

The woman's once-blue dress was moss-green from the hem up, as though she dragged the ground with her as she moved. She had a thin brown blanket around her shoulders. Something moved under it. When it came into sight, Helen gasped despite herself, then coughed as her lungs rejected the wet air she had just pulled into them.

The baby was small. Smaller than Helen could have imagined. The woman held it in the dip of one fragile arm, jostled it up and down in a quick rhythm. The woman looked down at it, then over at Helen, her eyes wild and desperate, her hands fumbling with the blanket. The ground felt loose under Helen's feet. She gripped the moist sock-ball in her hand. The voices from behind came closer and closer, Callie's mother yelling her full name, fury dripping from every syllable. Helen stepped toward the riverbank, waving frantically at the woman. But she stood, seemingly frozen to the spot, until the baby made a high noise that echoed in the clearing. Helen turned to the trees behind her, head high but her limbs trembling. Callie and Callie's dog and Callie's mother appeared through the leaves, huffing and swearing. Helen stood, defiant, her back to the river. Callie looked over her shoulder and Helen turned to follow her eyeline. But there was nothing to see across the water. Nothing to see at all.

Moses

The house is mercifully cool and dark until the women begin to move. Helen lights the lamps then walks around with a spool of tape around her arm like a bracelet. She twirls it and, every now and then, pulls a strip off with her teeth. She peels off old, curled pieces of tape from the little holes around the room and replaces them with fresh, checking for new holes or frass. She bundles the old pieces into her pocket where they form a sticky mass. She is always like this when they get home; unpacking and sorting immediately, while Juliana usually lounges on one of the dusty chairs with a mug of hot water, complaining about the blisters on her ankles where her boots have chafed, or slithers of cuts on her fingertips where the baiting hooks have nipped at her.

But tonight, they both move. Clothes are either put away or dumped in the washtub after a deciding sniff. There are only three rooms in the house, with the toilet in a slatted outbuilding in the backyard, so there isn't much to do, but still, windows are opened, the dishes that had been left out to drain a few nights ago are put away, the rucksacks are pinned to air on the line between the porch and the fence. Eventually, there is nothing to do but look at the thing in the basket. Juliana crouches down to it, her face close. She whispers, quiet as a footstep in the sand:

"Moses. We're home now. You're home."

Helen's shadow appears over her shoulder, cigarette smoke haloing the scene.

"What now?"

They look at each other, then around the small room. There are two battered leather chairs, a long and low wooden table of mismatched wood, metal shelves adorned with glass bottles, and a few open cupboards that hold the pans and knives and other kitchen things. In the end, they leave the basket on the floor, in the middle of the woven rug, where the orange and yellow pattern zigzags spread around it, like the sun in storybooks from the time before.

Juliana wakes alone in the bed. Light slices through the broken slats and onto the bedspread. One more thing for Helen. She always has some task, some small thing to focus on, something she can mend or fix, while outside the walls of their home the world falls apart. The dent in the bed at Juliana's side is still warm, but the house beyond is quiet, Helen no doubt up and at the day's tasks already. Juliana is alone. Almost. She pulls her nightshirt close to her body and steps out into the room.

Nobody on the chairs. Nothing on the rug. Her heart begins to race – she wouldn't, would she? – until she sees the basket on the kitchen counter and moves toward it, picking up a splinter in her haste. Moses lays naked in there, aside from the welded-on nappy. His eyes are still closed, his mouth a tiny puckered 'o'.

"Oh no, that won't do. That won't do at all. You'll catch a cold. Now, let me see…"

Juliana searches behind pans and moves boxes and opens drawers until she comes upon a tea towel, green and white check with a faded pattern of red flowers in the centre. She lifts Moses from the basket and gasps as his eyelids click up, the stubby lashes revealing faded blue eyes underneath. She laughs. She tilts him back and forth, down and up, watching the eyes close and open, close and open. After a time, she lays him back on the kitchen counter, careful to avoid the stovetop. She wraps the tea towel around him, then plucks a metal pin from her hair and gently presses it into the material, through and out, then in again, before patting down the cloth. She lifts Moses to her shoulder. Holds him tight.

Helen chops wood outside, watching Juliana through the window. She lets out a deep breath. Slings the axe above her head, then down again.

Juliana

When Juliana was younger, she met up with the girls from her class most weeknights, once their chores were done. Every day was the same, but the nights, at least, were different. At school they followed the routines slavishly; herbalism, first aid, foraging, fitness. Daylight hours belonged to their teachers, then their mothers, but the evenings back then belonged to the girls.

Juliana stretched and puffed her stomach out, as big as it would go, then sucked it back in again until her ribs poked. She half-listened to the girls babbling around her.

"I heard you can reverse it, but only on the same day. You have to get someone to suck it out, like with snake venom."

"But wouldn't they then get sick?"

"No – it goes in our bodies anyway, don't it? You just have to find another person willing to suck on your skin."

They laughed as Kelly Jones jumped up, planted her plump lips onto the freckled dome of Mimi Boardman's shoulder and sucked her cheeks in, leaving a red stain behind, the shadow of two lips around the faded scar. Juliana laughed too. But she knew that soon enough they would find a quiet place where they could press their lips to each other's bodies for real.

For some of the girls, it just happened that there weren't enough people to go around. Not by then. And so, they adapted. But Juliana had always known, since watching the nurse who had come to her visit her father every week. Something in the way the buttons on her uniform gaped, just a little, as she leaned over to feed him thin sips of water or tend to his burns. There was no skin on show, none at all. But Juliana would wake, warm and damp, with her cottons tangled around her and the flashing memory of the gaping buttons echoing behind her eyes.

Juliana watched the girls pair off from her usual place – the curved log that had fallen across the path, the thick bark grooves leaving wavy lines on the backs of her calves. It wasn't that she didn't want to go with them, she did. She wanted it in her body. In the swirling sensation low down in her stomach. In the pulse that made her clench her thighs together when one of the others came close and whispered in her ear. But she thought of her mother, alone with nothing but her pictures. The weight of loss on top of loss that dragged at her, ravaged her, all but destroyed her. If Juliana had no one to love, then she would have no one to lose. She puffed her stomach out again, and jabbed at the smooth, firm skin.

Now the evenings belonged only to Juliana and her memories. The girls from her youth scattered across the country in search of work, or hope, or simply to disappear. The nurse long gone. Her mother too. Juliana stared at the bottom of her empty glass. Alone. Just she'd always intended it. When she hadn't known any better. When she'd thought she would be able to cope.

She glanced at the people in the bar, but they were all coupled up, or in larger, rowdy groups. She passed over her money and dragged her jacket onto her shoulders. Her stomach roiled with the drink in there – some warm liquid pulled from a barrel around the back – and with each gurgle she pressed her hands under her vest, hoping to feel a flutter of something pressing back, something moving inside her.

She walked around the corner and down a thin alleyway with boarded-up shops either side of the path. She reached into her bra and took out the plastic-wrapped pill the barwoman had slid over with her change. Her legs began to tremble. She steadied herself against the wall then put the flat green tablet under her tongue.

The sickness came first, always the sickness. She bent over, vomited grains and rice and whatever putrid liquid she had been drinking onto the weed-riddled pavement. She wiped at the strings from her mouth then shuffled along the grimy wall before the other sensations kicked in.

Juliana knew nothing was really happening, she knew everything was the same, she knew it was all a trick. But she felt it. She felt her breasts throbbing under her cotton vest. She felt her feet, aching and swollen. Then the real high. The stomach. Engorged. Rippling. Life swirling through it. She peeled back her vest and watched, entranced, as small fleshy lumps fought under her skin. She cried, great heaving sobs, knowing that at any moment the drugs would wear off and she would lose it again, that she would be alone, again.

Moses

Juliana carries Moses around for a while, taking him to the windows, showing him the nooks and crannies of each carefully salvaged room. The steel shelving they'd pulled from a pile of rubble that was once home to dozens of brightly-lit shops. The chipped glass bottles they'd dug from the riverbed, shined and polished to catch the light. She keeps him close to her, patting and whispering all the while. Helen brings in the wood, sweeps the floor, fishes cobwebs out from the corners of high, cracked windows, pinches the rat droppings in a paper towel and washes her hands after tossing them out.

The two of them had tamed a stray cat once, hoping it might come and solve the rats for them. They had taken crumbs and leftovers and whatever they could spare to the front porch each afternoon, testing it. Tempting it. Closer, and closer, until it would feed from their hands. Its small paws were tiny, the claws sharp as needles pressing to flesh. It had come to them, every day for weeks. They had named it Luna because of the white circle of fur on its chest and had looked forward to seeing it, to having something that was small and soft and theirs.

But then, one of the bad times had come. When warning sirens pealed through the night. When fires burned for weeks.

When everything felt like it might fall apart. When it wasn't safe to leave their home for supplies. When they chewed on small pieces of shaved wood to try and drive the pangs away, to try and make every morsel count.

Luna had pawed and howled at the door.

Juliana had cried.

"We'll manage. Please don't. Please. We'll keep the bits we've been giving her."

"They won't make a dent."

"Neither would Luna, look at the size of her. Please. We can't. We just…can't."

"Fine. Let her be. But no more scraps."

Sighs and silences and metal forks scraped onto barren plates until things had eased. Meanwhile, Luna had continued to appear, for days. The tiny scuttling sound of her paws scraping at the door. The whining meowls that caused Juliana to leave the room and bury her head under blankets. Then one day, when they could have had food to spare, Luna didn't appear. Perhaps eaten by something bigger. Perhaps taken in by someone kinder. Perhaps just gone.

Juliana tells Moses the story of the cat with the moon on her chest and her greedy little paws, only in this version, the cat becomes a pet, that curls up warm on their feet every night and bats at the string they pull around the floorboards. Juliana fusses over Moses as she tells it, picking at the scuffed tufts that are left sprouting from the thin black holes in his scalp. Moses pouts, his eyes wide and fluttering, or lies in a peaceful slumber, depending on how Juliana holds him. She moves over to the door with him, peers out into the forest and gasps as she sees a flash of black and white fur.

"Luna! Luna! Come here, girl, Luna!"

She pushes back branches, not feeling the hard *thwack* as they bounce back onto her skin. She searches and calls, calls and searches, but whatever it is, is long gone. She walks back to the porch, her eyes stinging, her skin drenched in sweat and only then sees what she has done.

Moses.

Forgotten.

Face down on the boards with a band of aphids flitting around him. She shrieks as she flicks them away.

"No! Away with you. No!"

The tears come then. Thick and fat. She clutches Moses to her chest and cries and rocks and pats and soothes and then, almost by instinct, something she must have seen, or been told once, she pulls down the thin sleeve of her vest until her arm is out the other side, and her breast with it. She holds Moses to her. Shudders at his cold lips on her. Keeps him there anyway.

Helen appears from the treeline, roused by the shouting. She hurries, shooing away bugs from her face but stops when she sees Juliana. She moves forward then turns away, back into the woods, her hands trembling. She leans against a trunk for support and rustles through her pockets. She lights and takes a drag from a rolled cigarette. Then another, then one more. When it is done, she drops the stub to the dusty forest floor, and drives her toe into the flame until there's nothing left but a small patch of charred earth.

Helen

Helen wore the same jacket the others on her team did, a
faded blue denim with a set of wings stitched above the left
pocket, though she didn't know that she believed in angels,
or in God, or in anything at all. At first, part of the job had
been to scoop up others, try and convince them to join, to
give them a safe place to ride it out. Some had joined, but
most just wanted back on the streets, left with whatever small
comforts they had chosen for themselves. Others had taken
– greedy, selfish. Helen had quickly learned to lock up the
supplies, to not be taken in by a smile and a sob story. She
didn't make the same mistake twice.

Juliana hadn't been on Helen's patrol, someone else had
pulled her from the floor, cleaned her up. But her wails had
pierced the thin hostel walls until Helen gripped her paper
cup so tight it folded in her hands and spilled hot liquid over
her fingers. She'd pulled back the curtain, ready to snap,
until she saw Juliana. Her frame was beyond thin, and her
hair was cut too short, close against her head. Her skin was
blotched with crying, her eyes drowning in deep blue circles.
Her empty arms lay in her lap though she moved them side
to side, like something was held there. She blinked at Helen,
confused.

"I thought I— I had a— it was right here."

Helen nodded as she approached the bed.

"It's the drugs. Have you had that kind before?"

Juliana nodded and whispered something.

"What's that?"

"I said. Every day. I take them every day."

Helen pulled the flimsy chart from the end of the bed.

"Then I'm surprised we haven't met."

It took days for the effects of the drugs to fully leave Juliana's system. Days during which Helen cradled her, held her, bound her when she needed it. She had done it before, for dozens of women. There hadn't seemed to be anything particularly special about this one, not at the time. She was no more or less broken than the others they treated. Once the shaking and wailing and fighting had stopped, Juliana was quiet but calm. She was smooth and soft where Helen was not, the essence of her humanity slightly blunted from the stresses of her work, and the women's noises that picked apart her dreams at night. Juliana avoided the street work, said it was too painful. But in the hostel she tried her best, and the two women sat together in the evenings, sharing kisses and tentative plans. Perhaps another building, something they could pretend was more permanent.

They could have lived out their days there.

Could have done small, good things together.

If it hadn't been for the pregnant woman.

There were always rumours; whispers passed through the streets, reports of girls who'd swerved the injections, who had somehow made it on their own. But none had been seen – really seen – for years.

Groups usually lined the pathway leading to the hostel, stitching or hulling, laughing and talking, chairs and stools overflowing the cobbles and onto grass. That day, they were silenced. Hurried feet shuffled noiselessly as the woman was stretchered in. Juliana was in the rec room, mid-song, when she became aware of quick footsteps, of people rushing to doorways and a low, loud moan, like an animal awaiting slaughter.

The woman thrashed. Too heavy to be carried up the stairs, she was laid on a couch in one of the first rooms, the wet material of her dress clinging between her legs. Juliana stood in the doorway, her hand pressed to her mouth as the woman lurched up. Helen pushed past the gathered crowds and raced into the room. Pushed past Juliana without a glance. Pushed the woman back down again and yelled for the straps. Someone closed the door. The women slowly dispersed. Only Juliana stayed, with her ear pressed against the wood, pain flashing in her eyes. She made her hands into fists and dug them into her abdomen, not hitting herself, not exactly, but pushing, pushing, pushing in, feeling only her rib bones in return. She began to moan in unison with the woman, a bitter, howling wail.

Moses

Juliana is asleep, her thin legs curled up under the pale sheets. Her head rests only on her arm. The pillow that should be under her head is down on the floor at the side of the bed. Moses lies on top of it. Helen moves deftly, her bare feet noiseless on the floor. She pauses at the bedside, puts her face close to Juliana and feels the warm exhales of breath on her face. She watches the eyelids flutter and knows the images that will be there; a yellow sun, a blue sky, a pink baby – but real, alive, warm.

Helen picks up the plastic toy. The eyelids open. She rubs at the pale blue paint underneath them, and a fleck comes away. She presses the stomach and feels the hardness in there, some battery-powered thing that should no longer work at all, but still gives off a faint wheeze. She looks at Juliana. So peaceful in her sleep. She takes the toy away, from the room, from the house, from their lives.

The sun is bright and heavy, beating its way through the canopy but Helen is nearly done when she hears the noise. Juliana pounds through the forest, coming closer and closer.

"Moses! Moses!"

Helen wipes her dirty hands on her trousers, mops the sweat from her brow with her sleeve.

"Stop it, just stop it. You know it can't hear you. You know it wasn't real."

The women face each other, eyes wide and blurred. Juliana trembles, Helen stands firm. Juliana moves forward, fists flying, but Helen holds her back, holds her until the fight becomes an embrace.

Juliana sobs and falls to the floor, her hands clutching at the leaves.

Helen stays with her. Cradles her. Calms her. She has done it before, for dozens of women. They sit, rocking in the earth, grasping onto each other, listening to the sounds of the trees. Helen runs her hands up and down Juliana's arms, looks over her shoulder where small plastic hands reach out through the rough mound of earth. She will have to come back, to make a better job of it, when she has the time.

Juliana, Helen, Moses

And on the very last night – which won't be too long now – Helen will come here with a shovel, and she will dig. She will bring Moses back to Juliana and he will heal their pain, just a little, but it will be enough, and the three of them will sit together, and watch the colours dance in the sky, as they might have done in another time, in another life.

How to Dress a Rabbit
Clayton Lister

Before packing, we had warning sufficient – just – to eat a light breakfast. My younger brother Jake and I were lucky enough boys, so Mother had it, to be visiting our Granny Wallop. A holiday, she said. I had concerns from the off, she never before having used Granny Wallop's name in any but a cautionary context. Typically, "Ee, tha'd not be so swaimish, wi' thi Granny Wallop rearin' thee."

Nevertheless, my hope was that if not the same taxi we caught from the train station in Settle, then an ambulance would be returning Mother. For if she wasn't herself planning on heading all the way back home to Leeds, at least there in Settle she might be delivered of her third child in hospital. This was a hope washed clean away with her breaking waters.

Forget a place to give birth, I couldn't have imagined a dwelling more remote than Granny Wallop's. But wedged as it was into a hillside otherwise adorned with dry stone walls, mud and sheep only, better tumble down Wallops Roost than the backseat of a taxi. Our cabby certainly thought so. Slewing around those hairpin bends, it's a wonder we didn't lose the baby down a gorge.

Although any relief either our cabby or I felt upon arrival, Granny Wallop soon dispelled. For her brittle sheaf of white hair that had slipped its tie and eyes wild like flaming copper, she might have just dismounted that besom she came out wielding. If I hadn't been petrified at the sight of her, I'd have jumped back in the car. Cabby was off before Mother could pay him.

She'd given us boys more notice of our 'holiday' than she had her own estranged mother. And it seemed that only her being with child kept Granny Wallop from breaking that besom across her backside.She'd not be pregnant for much longer. Notwithstanding, with the same sublime indifference that Mother bore all adverse consequences of her own ill-planning, she waddled wetly across the cobbles into Wallops Roost. From across the threshold, "Thee mind Jake," she called over her shoulder.

As if Jake needed my minding. True, I was the elder by two years. But, commensurable with my deepening perennial state of anxiety, was envy of Jake's general obliviousness. In which respect, he clearly took after our mother.

We remained on the forecourt, and it was Granny Wallop who followed Mother's lead down the dark hallway, up the stairs.

"Ned, thee mind 'em both!" she barked over her shoulder.

I presumed she was talking to me. I presumed it was her mangy old black Lab she wanted minding. Clearly, between them there was no love lost. But no. She was talking to the Lab, which to my mind could mean just one thing. My mother had named me after her old dog. I felt some fraction less than honoured.

He, Doggy Ned, stuck his nose – his cold sopping nose – into my palm. I didn't aim a kick at him as Granny Wallop had, but he did move swiftly on to Jake. If it hadn't been for the steady drizzle that swirled, I most certainly wouldn't have followed them into the house. The smell of woodsmoke that emanated nauseated me. Furthermore, having followed, I found that its narrow, latticed windows admitted so little light, all the rustic impedimenta that was discernible might have been the stuff of witchcraft.

Yet, as upstairs our mother's grunts grew into moans, these in turn drawing into wails, there in the parlour Jake

coolly set to poking the fire. When he ran out of sweet
wrappers to send flaming up the chimney, he sat back on the
stone floor. Long before Mother's gritstone-rending screams
had subsided, I believe he was asleep. By the time the baby's
bawling had abated, I know he was. Because at the sound of
Granny Wallop's footfalls descending the stair, I had to shake
him awake.

At length, she stood silhouetted in the half-light of the
doorway. "Bring 'em through, Ned," she said.

The scullery at Wallops Roost was larger than the parlour
but only marginally less lugubrious. What light did find its
way in fell chiefly on a large dark-stained farmhouse table
— although we boys were sufficiently lit for Granny Wallop
to adjudge us, "Aye, reight clemmed." When we showed no
inclination to either confirm or rebut her opinion, "Well, ent
thee?" she demanded.

"Aye," I breathed.

"Reight, then. Say sooa."

From out of nowhere she then produced, of all things,
a rabbit. It would have been shock enough if the thing were
alive. I backed up against a dresser. Even Jake's jaw dropped.

"Ah dooan't approve o' tha mother," Granny Wallop told
us, courtesy of what exactly I'd not a clue. But she held the
rabbit up by its ears. "Squeezin' aht brats like… Ee, weel, ah
dooan't knaw!"

Thud went the rabbit on the table. Granny Wallop drew a
knife from a block. She splayed its hind legs and on the blade's
point deftly raised the soft skin between them. "It's a boy,
by't way," she said, rolling her eyes upward at the ceiling. She
flipped the rabbit on its side and slit it open. Its skin, as she
prised it from around its waist, sounded to my ears for all the
world like trousers splitting.

Jake pulled out a chair and scrabbled up.

"'Appy?" Granny Wallop asked.

I don't know that Jake was ever happy as such. Come to that, he was never sad, rarely angry, or much of anything, actually. Satisfied that he was settled at least, Granny Wallop turned on me.

"Ah dooan't s'pose thee knaw oo feyther is?"

The baby's? I had a fair idea. I suppose it was out of loyalty that I kept mum. Or happen it was that rabbit, emerging bloodlessly from inside its own skin and fur, that struck me dumb. It might have been a pair of trousers that Granny Wallop yanked off it – tight for sure, but they came off in one.

Her flaming eyes fell on Jake. He wouldn't have known or cared who the baby's father was. He only looked up, as much to ask why she'd stopped – or maybe, why she'd left the rabbit's socks on? For her part, Granny Wallop nodded knowingly and pulled the rabbit's ostensible jersey off, although, whilst able to tug its forelegs through its sleeves, had to leave its head inside itself. Which was exactly how Jake himself looked with Mother trying to pull him out of his jumble sale polo neck.

"Knaw oo tha feyther is?" Granny Wallop asked him.

Jake didn't even register the question.

"Thee?" she turned on me again.

I also was preoccupied. But my silence warranted a prolonged tut and hopeless shake of her head. Whilst interrogating us, Granny Wallop had been busy slashing either side of each of the rabbit's hind knee joints. In turn, she now poised each lower leg over the table's edge and snapped it off. The front legs she wrenched off.

"Shurrup, Ned!"

Doggy Ned had conceded defeat and stopped trying to jump up by now. With age, his legs were too stiff. But he was circling the table, whining.

Granny Wallop put the blade to the rabbit's throat, and leant on it. *Crack* went the rabbit's neck. Its head fell off. I felt faint but could not look away, slippery limp pink bag of guts that rabbit evidently was. Granny Wallop drew a line the length of its stomach. Out they oozed. I could smell them. Doggy Ned, too. As Granny Wallop teased those entrails on to the table, he began to drool.

"Ah ses to 'er," Granny Wallop said, "she's nooa mooare business rearin' children than beast in t'field." From the rabbit's ribcage, she scooped out its organs one by one. Each, as it came, she tossed to Ned. "Tho' 'appen she do tek 'er pleasure like un."

Ned wouldn't have made long-stop in a Doggy Veterans Second Eleven. He could not catch. But he lapped each organ up from where it splat. I took no joy in watching. I couldn't but watch him slaver and chomp.

"Tek it!" Granny Wallop startled me. "It's lucky. Or so folk say." She was talking to Jake. "An' thee lad are gawn t'need it."

Jake's hand shot out across the table. Apparently for my benefit he held aloft his prize of that discarded be-socked foot he had been eyeing. While Granny Wallop rinsed the rest of the rabbit in the sink, he claimed its head and pelt, too. He donned them like a glove puppet. "Nyerrr. What's up, Doc?"

In my stomach, the metallic taste I had been swallowing hard these past few minutes all at once rolled to a boil. I made it to the door but it was a stable door. I'd never seen one before, and in my confusion could not fathom its latches.

I had to jump to reach, then hang doubled over the door's lower-half so as not to spatter the scullery floor.

Granny Wallop waited for me to finish, then, having flung open that lower-half herself, marched me over my mess into the yard. As she did so, "Ned Wallop! Thee animal, thee!" she hollered. I dropped to the cobbles fully expecting a kick in the side. But again, wrong Ned, for Doggy Ned it was who yelped.

Granny Wallop disappeared back into the scullery. I looked up through my tears and the rain to find him, Doggy Ned, lapping up my vomit.

Jake, all the while, was laughing like I'd never heard Jake laugh before – like he might die of laughter.

Ned smacked his jowls and ambled over to where I sat in my puddle. He set about my face. Holiday? Wasn't a holiday supposed to be a treat? Beaches, a donkey ride and stick of rock? This weren't going to be no holiday.

The remaining hours of that our first day at Wallops Roost passed like years. Geological epochs turned in the time it took for gloomy day to enter darker night. And for want of any motherly reassurance, preoccupied as mine was with tending to a bairn that nobody wanted, my mind strayed, stopping at a place of some greater dismal wonder than real life had delivered us.

On arrival at Roost, I had discerned evidence of witchcraft, you may recall. In the hallway, a knobbly-fingered tree's branch served as coatstand to a long, black cloak. Upturned on a rack, also of greenwood, sat knee-high boots of cracked leather. Granted, nothing so archetypally witchy as a pointed hat, although a mannequin's head quite chilled my blood. Woven from twine, this sat where in other hallways a lamp might have, sporting motorcycle helmet and goggles.

Wider inspection of property had in no way allayed my suspicions of unnatural interests. At rest in the parlour, I found a spinning wheel and handloom. Active, they would weave nightmares. Oh, and Jake's compulsion to pedal! Presiding on the landing, a grandmother clock – what else! – solemnly meting out the seconds to her chimes of mocking laughter. "An hour? But a quarter, lad! Ding-ha-dong...!"

Honestly, though. That scullery beat all. The depraved rituals of butchery it would have witnessed. Acts unspeakable. Hooks hung from the rafters. Chopping boards all stained. Knives of every length and blade type ceremoniously arrayed. Brutal cleavers, forks with fearsome prongs. Tongs for holding squirming screaming victims in flame. Viciously spiked tenderisers. A mincer clamped to the table's edge, so robust it could grind bones. Human bones! And shelves laden with jars of salted, oiled, pickled and chutnied unthinkables bearing testimony to all, mutely.

In bed, Jake's blissful rest alongside me was no better protection against these fancies than his lucky rabbit's foot. That sat atop our bedside drawers. I was only grateful Granny Wallop had decreed Bugs' head remained in scullery until 'tret'.

But when at last black night lifted, it was not courtesy of day. Cloud dispersed to flood the room with the light of a swollen moon. So bright was it, I would have sworn blind that same heavenly body had never hung over our estate back home. Not, do understand this, that the prospect of illuminated wilds beyond Roost's window was any kind of draw to me.

I heard the creak of bedsprings. Was it Granny Wallop? Surely not? It surely was. The click of her door's latch and a squeal of hinges sent me underblanket; the groan of landing's floorboards scrabbling deeper still. I might have been a rabbit myself, gone to ground.

It wasn't our latch that lifted next, though. Opposite our door, it was Mother's. Granny Wallop stole into her room, then out again, no words exchanged. The rhythm of our mother's snoring missed not a beat.

Footfall on the stair then.

In time, beneath our room, the latch of scullery door lifted. She opened that door, our Granny Wallop, and what for if not to venture into the night?

I flew from my bed then alright, no fear of waking Jake. He slept as log-like as our mother, always.

'Patio' would be too grand a designation for the concrete area out back of Roost. So too 'garden' for the mud it gave onto. Cloaked and booted, through this mire Granny Wallop squelched on bandy legs toward gated paddock. Good! She might proceed into hills beyond the paddock for all I cared, never to return. Mount her besom and be quicker about it.

Some way short of hills, however, she stopped and shrugged herself out of that heavy cloak of hers. It fell in a pool of deep blackness about her boots. Disrobing at all, I would have thought odd, but outright alarming, under her cloak she was starkers! There was no mistaking this. Skin as white and bright as the moon itself, from neck to loins, slabs of heavy muscle swathed our Granny Wallop's back. She'd the rear end of a rhino.

And then, whatever unseen bundle she had been clutching to her chest all this while, she raised. You'd have thought she was showing it to the moon. Showing or offering. How the wet slap of eyeball on glass didn't alert her is a wonder. More naked than she was for lack of boots, that wriggling bundle was only our baby brother.

"Jake," I said.

Nothing.

"Jake!" Still nothing.

Fetch mother, Ned! I thought, but could no more move than wake Jake.

Happen, no need. Bairn evidently sufficiently moonwashed, our Granny Wallop re-baffled that freshly squeezed-out brat, brats as we of Mother's offspring all were, in her own milkless dugs. And I will say this for the old woman. Re-cloaking, she might have lain him in the mud. Squatting deeply, her balance was something. Dexterity, too.

Oh, my relief when she rose, re-cloaked, to squish back home. But as she proceeded, I began to take in the junk on the yard below. A tower of wattle holding cages. Not so alarming. Doors open, they stood empty. But erected in a clearing on the yard's far edge, a roasting spit. What was that there, but an outdoor oven? It must have been. It had a chimney.

As for the wrought iron tripod in opposite corner, from which hung only a cauldron, well! As if confirmation of witchery was needed at this point. It was big enough to boil a bairn in easily. The entire litter of us, I shouldn't wonder.

But no need to cage this infant whilst building a fire for whichever preferred cooking method. Glinting coldly atop a slaughtering block, a hatchet. Oh, my giddy aunt.

I swooned.

Had she seen me? From where mud met yard, she stood looking up. I daren't withdraw from the window. I daren't breathe. I could see the angry spangle in her eyes.

Now Jake stirred. He didn't wake, of this I was sure, but in sleep sent a spidering hand out from under blanket for his lucky rabbit's foot. I shifted my eyeballs sidelong, which was all the movement I did dare, and saw him pressing it to his cheek. He sighed.

I flinched to hear our mother cry out from across the landing then. Only the one word, but roared loud enough to knock the moon out of orbit. "Mother!"

Outside, Granny Wallop heard. And she'd seen me now, no doubting. For when our eyes locked again, she held mine fast.

Even whilst she did, she raised bairn, not overhead, as she had in paddock, but face-height. And, curiously, because I had thought her more likely to take a bite out of him, she kissed him. Ever so lightly, but she did. Gaze hard on me, she laid her lips on his forehead.

"Mother!" ours roared again, from her doorway this time. "Where is 'at bairn? Damn you, tha relic, thee!"

Down below, Granny Wallop, winked at me, swaddled her grandchild up in her cloak, gave Doggy Ned a steer out the way with boot and proceeded into Roost.

Memory Chip
Helen Nathaniel-Fulton

While we few women wait, finely poised like runners on their blocks, a signal is given that there's a hold up. We have to stand at ease again. It's rare but maddening when this happens: we were ready! *Dear God, what am I doing here in this country, in this place, at this moment?*

It was my choice. I came to West Germany in 1978, more than a year ago, to make a life in Europe's split state, but the longer I stay, the more disjointed I feel. Even my name is different here: I'm no longer Helen but 'Helena', pronounced He-lay-naa. I'm in the more desired, richer, capitalist half, but I'm always waiting in grim places and doing grim things...

Once a month, as I'm incapable of being anything other than law-abiding, I stand in a queue at the main Police HQ in Tuebingen, a town close to Stuttgart. The Polizei building is brutal and utilitarian, but the town itself achingly beautiful, trapped in another time much like Heidelberg. On the banks of the river Neckar, its tall, elegant buildings, a medieval church and fairytale castle reflect alongside trailing willows in green waters; flowers tumble out of window boxes; church bells toll; cobbled lanes twist and wind. Tourists love it.

But, every month, as a foreigner wishing to live here, I must find time to 'sign on'. I smile inwardly as I think about it: apparently, the Government needs to be sure I'm not wandering about the country willy-nilly, not a commie, not a political terrorist. They want useful incomers in stable situations. As a student, I qualify to stay: when I no longer have a student Ausweis or card, I will need to prove I have a suitable, permanent job to remain.

It's always a long queue. The University here enrols tens of
thousands of students annually, from all over the world. We
who wait are blurred, distorted shapes reflected in mirror-
polished grey tiles. The queue spans the corridors of the
police station, where even the desk officers are armed. We
students are not alone, but interspersed with Gastarbeiter,
the 'Guest Workers' from Eastern Europe. They need to sign
each month too. Keen to benefit from the booming economy,
they work hard to send money home to better their own
and their families' lives. You soon feel 'guests' is too cosy
a description for them: they need work, German factories
need workers. Ergo, they are tolerated if they contribute to
production and cause no trouble. But they live in run-down
accommodation in questionable areas of the towns and cities
or in crowded hostels. The police eye them with deepest
suspicion, monitoring their movements with extra care.
Foreign students are treated with a little more graciousness –
we are educated at least, a cut above the others – but we all
sign the book each month and feel… Apart… Temporary.

Anyone would be entitled to ask why a young woman
from Wales is moving from foot to aching foot in this motley
queue. Now approaching my mid-twenties, I possess a
Masters Degree in History and a Diploma to manage archives
and read/conserve crumbling documents – I could already
be employed. I would have to explain it's an old, old story:
I came here out of love for my German partner, Micha.
We've flipped roles neatly – he was a foreign student at
Aberystwyth. Meeting early on in his time there we were
soon inseparable, bodies, minds and souls happily entangled.
Friends called us *Michaandhelen* as if we were one entity. For
now, I'll just say he is a complex but charismatic person,
a brilliant literature/philosophy student and dedicated

musician. He is effortlessly popular, never worries, lives in the now. Always tells me I worry too much.

"R-e-l-a-x, honey," he says. "I love you. As long as we're together, we'll be fine. It will all work out."

His English is fluent, with a hint of Marlene Dietrich.

It was a leap over a cliff edge to come here... Technically, I suppose I 'dropped out' – a little late in the day! – afraid suddenly of ending in a cellar endlessly cataloguing documents, breathing in a different kind of dust to ancestors who worked in local mines and brickworks in South Wales. My weakness is to follow a path of least resistance – after school, university; jobs in vacations to supplement my grant and finishing with not just a degree but a useful qualification, leading straight to a career. Just as panic set in, a new beginning and possibilities opened up. I told myself I wasn't running away: it was a chance to step off what had begun to feel like a treadmill. I whipped myself up: *come on, Helen! Decide. You can improve your O-Level German quickly and once fluent, you can find something congenial to do, surely? Just decide.*

Micha pressed me hard, I convinced myself and I leapt. Though we stay in attractively cheap student lodgings, we must both take temporary jobs, for several months at a time, as we have no other income. Micha explained from the outset the best paid 'casual' work is usually in factories – where I will work alongside the Gastarbeiter. They and I are meant, it seems, to be thrown together, to form strange symmetries and perhaps relationships for a time. They say work makes you free: I wondered what it would do for me...

A sudden movement from our supervisor jolts me back to the now. The arm half-raised signal is given: get ready, get set. We all focus and tense again, weight forward, ready to push off with our toes. The air around us seems to hum, our pulses to beat in sync with the regular, rapid beeps of the monitors. A flash of humour makes me glad we're not attached to those machines – the needles would strain into the red section, the glass screens crack. The tension reaches unbearable levels until the signal of an arm raised means 'Go!'

We're supposed to be working as a team, but each of us just wants to get it over now, do her part and get the hell out. And yet our heads rise as one when we sense the signal is about to be given. Yes: the last person has left the room, and we're off.

When you see scenes of surgery on TV or in film – the more realistic versions – you never get a sense of the speed or brutality involved. You certainly don't imagine the volume of blood, or the fact surgeons are like a gorged Henry VIII, carelessly tossing bits of bone and tissue to the floor as they whizz through another meaty banquet so fast it makes you wonder if they get paid per patient or by the hour. Those floors are no longer covered with herbs and straw, and if the person swabbing has been unable to keep up with the flow, the blood pools are surprisingly large and slick. Worse, if the operation has been a very long one, the stuff seems to get glued to the tiles and ever harder to shift. But we are protected, of course, or, rather, the room is protected from our contamination. Latex-gloved, booted and masked, each one of us thinks of nothing but hitting the deadline and how to ignore the irritation of sweat running in rivulets down our skin and into our eyes. I blink away its sting now, and note that though muffled, the smell of blood is metallic, sharp and rotten at the same time, as if it's already begun to turn under hot lights. The conundrum facing us humans is we think, we feel, I suspect we even have souls: but if we come trailing clouds of glory, we are also meat. In these secluded places, our inner secret is revealed. Our bodies are opened to vent their stinks. Here, meat is cut up and rots from the moment it gapes raw to the air.

More than a dozen rubbery arms are flailing, wiping, scrubbing, spraying every surface in the greenish white light – we've become an oversized octopus, tentacles waving underwater. I re-focus, follow what I've been told and finish at the same moment as the others. We are a cleaning production line! Another signal, and we're out. There's an odd satisfaction to it, as if synchronised swimmers have executed the most intricate routine in perfect formation, but my lungs labour, my muscles scream and though I could drink a river, only salt water dries on my lips. The door *swhooshes* shut on the pristine silence, the crystalline clinical cleanliness. Only ten minutes are allowed between operations, not a second more, and we go out as we came: through a back door into the sordid disposal area. What is astonishing is no one sees us, and no one even imagines us. That makes us less than ghosts. Mad though it sounds, I think the staff here also think it's like the TV, like the films: they probably think these areas are magically self-cleaning. They're not. Nothing in the world of humans is. We are allowed to rest, of course, if there is a lull. Allotted our own little room, bare and neon-lit, in which we wait. Naturally, there are strict timetables, but sometimes several operations overrun, and we endure a stagnant period.

You know, I think I prefer when the times are closer together. I think I'd rather work till I drop. We are all female, you see, and I'm the only one who isn't Turkish. My co-workers all look the same: not a lick of dark hair peeping from beneath their headscarves, olive skin, plump bodies wrapped in black drab, faces oddly middle-aged even if young, skin like apples left too long in a winter store. Almost all have bad teeth, and every one is haloed by a visible odour of salt-fresh perspiration mingling with old sweat. Am I? There's no mirror in here, so we can't see what we look like. I can't look into the black mirrors of their eyes as they will not meet mine: the unfriendliness is palpable. The women speak their own tongue and pretend I'm not there. Such an odd feeling: if no one sees or imagines you, if you can't look at yourself and no one speaks to you, how long before you don't just suspect, but believe, you're not there? Worse than the alienation, however, is the knowledge they want me to fail. I know they want me gone because I make them even more uncomfortable than they're making me. I'm the foreign body.

The smartly-dressed and coiffed German woman in personnel who hired me knew how it would be. She frowned. Heavens: was I sure? It just didn't seem right! Only the euphemistically named guest-workers, the Gastarbeiter could, would or should do this work. She leant forward and confided that such work was given to Turkish women who had no education, spoke very little or no German, and were earning valuable Deutschmarks in the only way they could to send home. *One had to admit they were Eseln*, she whispered – *real donkeys: they could carry any burden without buckling or complaining and plod on forever.* She shook her head and her hair didn't move, although her slick pink lips did. Words formed like dirty steam out of those lips. *They are not like you, like me! They don't feel things as we do. Please believe me: I know them.*

I couldn't face challenging her, but explained patiently in my neat, but still schoolgirl German, that I'd arrived too late to get any of the better summer jobs, and I needed to earn. I told her I'd be very grateful to be taken on and wasn't at all afraid of hard work. She stared at me, and her expression said: 'My God, how naïve are you!' Of course, that made me more determined. I wanted to show her I could do it. Then, of course, I wanted to show them. In this second, however, I don't know where that determination has gone: I just feel like weeping. Nothing prepares you for being so tired, so overheated, so – dehumanised. I'm very good at hiding my feelings, however, and I sip at the water cooled by a hot, humming machine, pretend to read my book and try not to shift in the chair. If I do, they'll know I'm aching!

Suddenly, there's a light, electrifying trill of a fingertip on my bare arm and it makes my heart skip. I look up, straight into eyes that aren't black at all, but a rich, moist-earth brown. With another shock, I see the woman is young – maybe even younger than me – but there are deep lines between her brows, and apart from the life in her eyes, the rest of her looks worn as a threadbare rug. The others are talking animatedly about something, and she rolls those dark eyes. When she speaks, her voice rustles and her German is execrable. We both know we mustn't look at each other and speak like ridiculous Hollywood gangsters out of the sides of our mouths. "Was dein name? What you called?"

I blink, swallow and clear my throat quietly. After so many hours of silence, I've forgotten what my voice sounds like. I have to force it out to whisper back: "Helena."

"I Sofia."

We both glance nervously at the others, but their discussion becomes heated, and they take no notice of us.

"Too hard, this work. You student? You German girl?"

"Student, yes, but British… English."

She looks at me now as if I've journeyed from Saturn's rainbow rings.

"But why? Why you work here? Ist nich gut."

"I must work. My boyfriend is a student too. We have no money."

She smiles and shakes her head slightly. I can see she doesn't believe me. Before I can think and stifle the stupid question, it comes. "Sofia, why do you work here? So far from home?"

The lovely eyes grow darker and the smile slides off pale lips like bright blood wiped up silently and swiftly from the floor.

"Same as you! Money. Father die, I have no brother. I old sister— only me to work. Big family. My mother say must come here." Her eyes stare at the table, but she inclines her head slightly towards my book. The words are beginning to flow. "I no read like you. No school."

A tear wobbles on dark lashes, threatens to spill but she expertly draws it back, glancing again at the women. One of them now looks fit to bust, and all are waving their arms as we do when we're cleaning. The Kraken wakes, and strangles itself with its own tentacles. Better than them extending out to me. To us.

"They no like you."

"But why?"

"You take money of Turk woman. They think you—what is word?— not strong. You go soon. Not... not like us."

I can't help it: something combative stretches in me.

"I work as hard as all of you!"

She smiles, and it's a sad smile. We become aware the noise level has abated a little, and one of the women is staring in our direction. Actually only one of her eyes stares at us: the other points in a different direction. Does it mean she can

46

watch the door and us? Sofia whispers almost inaudibly: "We talk later. I try speak English."

I look down intently at the page in front of me, but the German supervisor saves us by opening the door and spitting out: "Let's go— theatre five, then two. Schnell!" He looks at the women with breath-taking contempt, but ignores me. Of course he does – I'm not there. He signals with fingers. "Understand? F-I-V-E and T-W-O."

Two weeks later, and someone I know has found me a job replacing her as a cleaner in the Post Office. For some reason, they prefer to employ Germans – and I'm as close as, so it makes no difference. As jobs go, she says it's hog heaven: the clerical staff has gone home, you do the offices, corridors and toilets in peace and at your own pace. An added perk is you get to eat practically for nothing in the canteen. Best of all, if you work hard and fast, you can even sneak off to the toilets you have made super-clean to escape into a book. It's shorter shifts and slightly less pay than here, but that no longer matters a jot: once you've been in the dark, dirty and terrifying basement, the meanest room in the upper house looks palatial. Of course I have to save face: I tell Sofia and she in turn explains to the women who were starting to unbend a little that I enjoyed working with her and them, but I've found another job. It goes without saying it's a better job, so I don't say it. Even as I speak, I despise myself for lying. Truth is, if I had to go hungry I couldn't work here another hour. I know it. They all know it. They pretend to be supremely uninterested, though the least friendly of them can't help smirking. Maddeningly. But I no longer care, and, tired as I am, I'm riding the waves. I avoid Sofia's eye as I head for the door: it's the kindest thing I can do. I undress

and shower in an echoing, empty locker room – the others
have stayed to work another half-shift, as it's more money
– and my relief is as delicious and cool as the water. When
I'm finished, sparkling clean, solid and free, I pass the coats
and jackets hanging in a row like bagging, shed skins. I know
which one is Sofia's, and I place a hazelnut 'Milka' bar – a
rare, favourite treat I've seen her slip secretly and greedily
piece by piece into her mouth – in her pocket. Wrapped
around it is a note telling her if she wants to practice English
or reading, I'd be happy to meet her whenever we have spare
time. I know she'll guess immediately who's left it and will
keep it hidden if she has to find a sympathetic friend to read it
to her. I've written it in capitals in English and German, and
made the address and telephone number very clear. But I've
begun to suspect she lives with the evil-eye woman (whom
she manages later to tell me is her aunt), and something tells
me she won't get in touch.

I am lucky enough next time I approach the student
employment service to get a job in the Mercedes Benz Factory
at Stuttgart. This is hitting the jackpot, as it pays the highest
wages of all. The journey from Tuebingen is a pain though
as there is a 4 a.m. rise to catch the bus for the early shift
that starts at 6 a.m. – but, after all, it's only for ten weeks. I
must keep that thought. Today is my first day and already the
reality of life on the factory floor is slapping me in the face. I
am like an insect on a pin. Splayed and displayed. Transfixed,
exposed, wings stretched paper-thin. I'm trying to imitate the
discreet stillness of the recently dead, but all the observers
know I'm very much alive, a splash of white and summer
colour on a darker background. At least I am alive, I suppose,
if in temporary stasis. And yet… perhaps I'm worse off than

any captured butterfly, for I am aware of the gaze of dozens of eyes in a neon-lit, surgically-clean, no-bloody-hiding-place restaurant that smells of Germany: potatoes, cabbage and vinegar, roast sausage and curry powder.

Here I sit, alone, body curving into the ergonomically-shaped plastic chair. Even furniture is ruthlessly efficient here. Wood is unhygienic. Wasteful! This chair wastes nothing: it simply is and does its job to perfection. Meanwhile, I'm waiting with impatience for the strong coffee and steaming plate of sausages before me to cool a little. Yes – here I am in very post-war Deutschland: run like clockwork and awesomely affluent, finally ueber alles in economic if not the military terms it wanted! A country getting rich instead, in which there is money for nothing: money on tap... well, not quite! In fact, if you're at the bottom of the tall heap, you have to work 'til you want to sob with exhaustion, just as you would anywhere on earth.

Still, due to a seemingly inexhaustible demand for gleaming Mercedes cars, there is at least money galore for manual labourers and students, for those desperate enough to do one of the jobs the robots find too unpredictable. Jackpot cash for humans prepared to perform the allotted tasks over and over on hundreds of dry metal skeletons until every brain cell and nerve begins to beg for the end of an eight-hour shift. Tempting rewards for someone like me who won't eat unless she makes those little tweaks that need a human eye and judgement on a fast-moving production line... but no brain function: oh, definitely no brain activity required or desired. Here, on the production line, your most vital human organ is deliberately starved of oxygen, and I feel the sluggishness of mine as it crashes into gear now and tries to size up the problem.

Male eyes: *there's the rub*, as Shakespeare would have said. Eyes black with red lust, the ones to fear most! Others treacle-brown, melting with a warmer, more sentimental desire: eyes to look into while real sugar burns and Gypsy violins play. The rest flash amber, inviting an answer, spark like plugs in an engine and then… Wherever I am in the factory, I feel those unswerving stares of still young men from Eastern Europe and from Greece, Yugoslavia: men separated from wives and girlfriends, lonely and horny and hot as hell. Bored half unto death. Living (existing!) in hostels that make cheap motels look like the Dorchester. Men. Staring. Genuinely believing a young, liberated Western woman must be easy meat. Promiscuous. The only question is: which one of them will approach me first? It has to happen soon. The tension is terrible.

I know looking down at my food will not help. Pretending to read my book won't help. My skin is slightly tanned, but they will see the flush shining through as I've scraped long blonde hair back off my damp neck into a bun. You can't cover up too much as it's fiercely hot, but I'm doing my best by wearing a baggy T-shirt and a mumsy cotton skirt with a wallpaper flower pattern. But none of it will help. To believe anything else would be the illusion of Hope versus Experience. They can still see a bloom of youth on skin, those men, the poke of firm, nervous-tipped breasts when I have to breathe out. They can gauge the length and shape of a hidden leg. They've had a lot of practice. They may not have letters after their name, but that's their area of expertise.

The anger rises: I'm being stared at like some pin-up picture, an object for lust, disrespected though I've done nothing to merit this. Why am I fair game? If any man looked at one of their sisters like this, they would tear out his liver.

My cheeks must be hot to the touch now. Fuck them all!
I have to eat after seven hours up and six working and no
appetite for breakfast. Until I get my pay cheque, this is so
cheap it's almost free, and I have to sit somewhere to eat it!
Christ! To the hottest inner circles of hell with them! And
yet… I'm bolting the food down now, swilling the coffee,
annoyed by my cowardice, by the fact I'm giving in, but
prepared even to spend the rest of my longed-for break in the
toilets. It's cool and quiet there, and I can read my book. As
I'm about to push back the chair, my eyes still demurely cast
to the floor, a body plumps down opposite me. I have to look
up.

The man searches my face. I decide he is in his mid-
twenties, lanky; so tall he'll always stoop a little. His hair
is the colour of chocolate, his eyes hazel. His expression
is serious, but he has an attractive smile that reveals the
regulation bad teeth of the Gastarbeiter. The euphemistically
named 'Guest worker': God, what a cruel joke! Unwanted
but essential factory fodder fuelling an economic revolution,
more like! A slave labour force sanitised by being well
paid and legal, but still utterly despised by its superior,
commanding hosts. Germans have made this clear to me:
I'm different, of course. They're glad to have me and are
immensely impressed I speak German well. One day I could
be like a German! They don't tell me how pleased they are
that I'm as blonde, healthy and Aryan as they are.

"Boris. My name is Boris. You?"

His German is the usual pidgin type that people make
such fun of. I try to clear my throat, which is suddenly very
dry. To walk off is impossible after a lifetime of being urged
to be polite, always to remember one's manners. "Helena."

"Pretty! You are pretty, I think, but too serious. You are
English, I heard, and young. You shouldn't be here. Student?"

I can't help but stare, though I quickly close my lips.

"Yes. I'm a student. Well, sort of! It's easier that way. I really came here to be with my boyfriend."

He leans forward. His eyes have green flecks in them. They are lovely. They darken a little. Will my reference to being involved with someone be enough to send him away? Will he think I'm just saying it? My stomach curls into a knot and I wish I hadn't eaten after all. He looks angry.

"Your friend... he lets you work here?"

"Yes, of course!" I smile. I can't help it, but my face feels stiff. "He works here himself, but on the other site. We need the money."

"To live?" I nod firmly and look him directly in the eye.

"Yes. To live. To eat!"

He returns my nod. This is not going the way I expected, and I feel more uncomfortable than ever. I know the other men are still staring. I can feel the beams searing into me. I'm amazed marks like cigarette burns aren't appearing on my bare skin. The level of tension has been tightened up, like one of the wheel nuts on the assembly line. Everyone is waiting to see what happens next. I'm waiting to see what happens next. I can't explain it, but I don't want to run away anymore – I want to keep talking to the young man opposite me. I think he senses it, as he smiles widely. This time it's a real smile, a one hundred percent grin.

"I work to send money for my wife Anja and my family to eat. If I work hard, we can get a better house. More land. Better land. Then I go home. My mother is widow and my youngest sister live with us too. I have two sons. Beautiful boys. I show you a photo later."

Now I don't know what to say.

"My sister— she wants to be a student. She is clever. Read all the time, like you."

I have no words. He leans forward and puts a large, roughened hand on top of mine. I'm paralysed. I couldn't stir now if someone tossed a grenade into my lap.

"You smoke. I saw you outside."

"Y-y-yes."

"You come out now. We sit on the steps. We smoke together. Those others" – Boris glares at the men who are still openly or surreptitiously watching us – "Turks!"

He looks about to spit, but sees the look on my face and shrugs instead. "Bastard Turks... They treat women like cattle. So you come out with me now. Then they think you are mine, you have been taken. They will leave you alone."

It takes me some time to reply. My voice sounds as if my vocal cords are being squeezed. "Why?"

He misunderstands, frowns. "I just tell you! They will think you are my girlfriend— meine Frau— they leave you alone. Men, they can go to a woman on her own— but not if she has a man. They can see then you have a man."

This time my smile is involuntary but a little desperate. "I mean, why are you doing this... Boris? What... what benefit, what good can you get from it?"

As he beckons with an inclination of his dark head, I get up to follow him out into stifling smoke-tainted summer air. We blink in the sunshine. Everything is metal, the colour and smell of fresh coin. It stinks of burning metal out here. We sit. The metal staircase burns through the cotton of my skirt. I wince and fidget, and I really am now gasping for a cigarette. Boris lights two for us. But I can distinguish the heat of the stares from the metal branding my buttocks and legs and from the sun's rays at full power... I sneak a look as I relax and find his plan seems already to be working: the mood has changed. The few men out smoking in groups on different levels of the staircase or leaning against a nearby wall are less interested in me. They have seen that Boris and I have made a connection… The thwarted male sex gaze will need to turn elsewhere.

"It's because of my sister. I think, what if my sister had to be somewhere like this?" He frowns. "Or my Anja? Not that I would let them, dear God! But what if they had to be annoyed and insulted by Turks? I am a proper Christian man. Do you understand? While you are here, working here, I am your friend. You will be safe. My good friend here is Polish— Andrzej. He does the same. You will meet him. If I am not here, he will look after you."

Mesmerised, I nod. I know he's telling the absolute truth and wants nothing from me. There isn't even a sigh of wind, and the staircase is as solid as anything on earth can be, but it feels as if it's swaying. I have never felt as safe as this. To him – so natural and logical: to me, a revelation. I feel embarrassed to admit that, but I must or be dishonest. It's also embarrassing that my eyes are filling up and my throat is closing. I blink and I swallow hard, drawing deep on the cigarette. He returns the nod, and stretches his impossibly long limbs. His strong but very tired limbs. Now I'm so ashamed of how I judged him, I can't bear to look at him. In weeks I can count on my fingers, I'll be gone: how long will his sentence be? Will his beautiful boys know him again when he returns?

"Good! Now tell me about your home— do you miss it? And I will tell you about mine and show you the photo… here…"

I stare at the slightly greasy, curling photo in my hand. The woman cradling two lumpy featureless infants is stocky and plain, face sketched roughly in tired lines though she must be only about twenty. The boys gaze up at her like little idol-worshippers, however, and the dark eyes sending a message through the lens dance with love and mischief. I give up and let tears well, but the sun scorches my cheeks dry before they can drop. He frowns again, looks suddenly concerned.

"Careful… please! Is my best photo. My wife is beautiful, yes? And my boys— my boys! Anja says they look just like me…"

Do unto others… I hand the photo back carefully. For the rest of my time here, he will protect me, and I will do my best to encourage him not to stay here too long, living through a nightmare instead of waking up to his dreams.

Today, the sun could melt the hair on your head, and it's exciting the other women in the house where I live. Their voices rise in pitch as they talk of driving to a mountain lake at the weekend to bathe alternately in solid heat and ice-cooled waters. Then the sound of laughter recedes like an echo as they run upstairs to delve into cupboards. They'll find what they're looking for, and I smile to think of how the paint-blob-splash bikinis, the creased and slightly musty summer clothing, will whirl into the air and drop into heaps on the floor. To me, pearl-pallid, the heat signals months of discomfort. More importantly, however, it heralds the money-making season has come again. When thunder rumbles in the distance, I imagine it's the Mercedes Benz conveyor belt calling me. Though I'm scanning the job columns in the newspaper for the area, I'm resigned to having to answer that call. Suddenly, my eyes widen and track back to an advertisement and my heartbeat – grown worryingly sluggish and blurred of late – quickens.

I don't exaggerate about the heat: in these landlocked foothills of the Swabian Alps, the summer months are so airless and oppressive that I visibly wilt. I'm drooping a little already, and I assume that's why my energy is draining away as if a parched vampire is gulping his fill. The good news is there are jobs available at Bosch, a local home appliances factory. I sit up straighter, as the key word – local – resounds in my head like the sound of a nail tapping on fine crystal. Local! And the ad says one can even choose one's shifts! This potential workplace, you see, clings to the skirt hems of the frumpy and utilitarian neighbouring town... but if I could get a job there, Reutlingen would look radiantly beautiful to me. It's only ten minutes away by bus.

I lick drying lips. I would earn two thirds or even less of the wages paid by Mercedes Benz, granted, but would escape another endless summer spent as a Hell-factory android. To have a vivid imagination isn't always a blessing: I feel a greasy swell of nausea at the thought of getting up for the early shift at 4.30, and, suddenly, I'm back on the dawn bus again. I'm one of the many miserable, jaw-cracking drones, spending my long, silent journey trying not to vomit up cold milk, the only breakfast I can tolerate at that hour. Staring down at the ad, I feel an actual swing of giddiness. What a joy it will be not to do the 4 a.m. rise, the dreaded bus journey to Stuttgart feeling nauseous and disoriented with lack of sleep. What a relief that, despite slightly lower wages, I'll not be a slave to that relentless conveyor belt.

I've never minded early rises: it's simply a part of life's rhythms: going to school, early lectures, rising for work. Because I accept this and am usually cheerful enough in the mornings, I tend to irritate my partner Micha, who's always grumpy until about eleven o'clock if he has to rise early. He wakes up as the day goes on, picking up a frenetic momentum and consuming various illicit substances we can't afford. He is developing a particular liking for pure hash and cocaine, far removed from occasional grass joints made to focus in on his music. He's done that ever since I've known him. But he shrugs off my worries; lives for the now; tells me to relax. More often now he listens. Then he listens to music, plays guitar and/or parties like a Dervish until three or four a.m.

This doesn't make for harmonious relations.

Oh, yes: helping Bosch keep the world's clothes whiter than white would definitely suit me better! I could still earn a perfectly decent sum without turning into a nagging, sleep-deprived, grease-monkey drudge, and it might well defuse the tension that builds between Micha and myself when lifestyles and priorities meet head on. So, on the day and exact time stipulated, I enter the personnel department at Bosch Electronics Company. There's a crowd, but it's clean and quiet as a hospital. Serene. Odourless. No smell here of thick black machine-blood, of sun searing through glass into metal and hot rubber. No ceaseless daemonic din in vast, unholy Miltonian halls. In this intimate, hushed atmosphere, one feels the need to walk quietly or whisper. Employees glide: cool, unruffled. None of them sport sweat patches on the backs and underarms of T-shirts; none are grimed with a slick of oil! I'm glad I've worn neat summer cottons, and that my German is pretty fluent.

Micha is happy to live on an overdraft the size of a developing country's debt. His bank thinks he's going to be a dentist, you see, and dentists here make unfeasible amounts of money. What he hasn't told them is he gave up the dentistry course after six months to study philosophy and the American Beat Generation. I know, however, and often wake sweating as I dream of what will happen when they find out. He's an extravagant and generous person with other people's money. It goes on booze, drugs, parties, his book and music collections... And gifts for me I usually neither want nor need. In many ways, he really is an overgrown boy: mundane things are worried about and paid for by grown-ups, by fuddy-duddies like our parents – such petty concerns have little or nothing to do with him! He thinks I'm hopelessly bourgeois to care, but the only way I can live with it is to make sure I earn enough for all our basic needs so we depend on that bank for nothing vital. He takes occasional jobs too, but at longer intervals now. Like everyone else in the so-called civilised world and in its star economy, we've become victims of our own material comfort. We're caught in a heavy downpour of rent slips and bills with only one leaky umbrella between us. Bills have to be paid! I'm terrified of owing money.

Waiting in a room at the student employment agency, I smile grimly as I wait with everyone else to be called through. For years, though unsure of his worth, my family has expected me to marry Micha, but I've always held back instinctively. Now I know in my heart there'll definitely be no wedding, even if we could surmount the (already outdated) hippy principles of clinging to so-called freedom – a 'freedom' that can be as restricting as the bourgeois shackles he fears. I don't want to give these thoughts too solid a form, but I do know the compatibility I imagined existed between us is a lunar illusion. Like blue moonlight, it can be romantic but also unsettling. It's a thing of no real substance, after all: cold, second-hand light powered by no life-giving core of earth and fire.

If I'm an adept at anything, it's holding that dawning realisation at arm's length, and I itch to push it away. But I must not keep doing this. I force myself to think about what the evidence says about our suitability. Our initial joy in each other may have been superficial, and now, tested by tougher circumstances, our basic personalities and attitudes to life have been revealed as too different. I know I'm starting to see him in a light as harsh as the strip-lighting in here, the year's rosy screen slipping away.

I have to pause my thought process at that point as I'm becoming tearful, and that isn't a good look for a job interview. Facing up to difficult thoughts isn't easy, taking action even harder when it feels there is a barrier of passive resistance. And we've been through a great deal and we've been together a long time. He assumes we always will be, no matter what. I'm the more realistic, but, then again, I come from a long line of dedicated reality-evaders. I've been brainwashed in an old-fashioned South-Welsh upbringing to regard breaking a commitment as being a sign of weakness, even degeneracy. So I don't want to think about what I would do if I have to leave him and the life we've built together – however precarious it might be. There's so much not to think about, it takes at least 90% of my energy, and that normally boundless resource is shrinking fast. I'm so busy taking care of mundane things and pretending to be fine that I don't stop to wonder why I'm so exhausted, or reduced to tears by things I'd normally shrug off.

Mercifully, for the next hour, I can't think of anything at all, since, along with the other hundred or so applicants for about twenty jobs, I have to go through a series of complex dexterity and memory tests. We're all bewildered, frankly: we've come to get factory work, not join MENSA. Part of me starts to enjoy the challenge, relishing how my reactions gear up for it, while the rest of me feels anger at being treated like an unthinking lab rat. It rapidly becomes clear to all of us that speech or language facility is of no importance in this silent place. What matters here, it seems, is response time, nimbleness of fingers and a near perfect visual memory. As we progress through the exercises, those who fail are escorted away. I'm mesmerised by the tasks, determined not to be beaten or get a low score. When I finally look up, I'm startled to find fewer than twenty of us are left. A little dazed, we are issued on the spot with clean white coats to put in neat, clearly numbered lockers. White-coated staff from the personnel department and the factory floor join us.

We are shown silently around, and are duly impressed by
the facilities. We're the chosen few, the winners. We're in.
We are given instructions to start the following Monday, and
released into natural light.

I sit comfortably on a highchair at a sort of workbench cum
desk, doing my job. The chair is at the exact right height and
so carefully designed I feel no pain, though I have to sit like
this for eight hours with three short breaks a day. The desks
are well spread out so no one can talk, even if they were
able or wished to communicate. Workers are here to do
their jobs and not chatter: nothing must break their pinpoint
concentration. Each desktop is individually lit, and when it's
dark or the sun doesn't shine into the rooms, we sit in lonely,
eerie haloes of light. In front of each of us is a circuit board
with holes punched in it. Into each hole, a tiny component
must fit and be connected to others. We have models to look
at, but we no longer need to. We were chosen for our ability
to memorise, after all, and we know each jigsaw pattern
by heart. We can fill one of the boards that are the brains,
nerves, veins and tangled guts of a machine in seconds. It
needs no conscious thought, and while we do it we become
like the things we're helping to build.
    I don't ask, naturally, so I don't know how the others
feel, but I find the rhythm of the work oddly comforting, and
I rock gently and sing softly to myself as I create machine life.
I croon a kind of lullaby to the rhythm of the soft mechanical
clicks. More and more it feels like being a priestess in a
temple of futuristic worship, performing an intricate set of
mysterious rituals. I feel my own brain shutting down as I
make these circuits fit to fire up. Increasingly, I find it hard
to ignore the fact something is very wrong with me, but I'm
sure if I can just focus totally on what I'm doing, it will act as

a kind of anaesthesia and I can still pretend there isn't.

As I attempt to focus on my work, sound and light rushes at me and then recedes, like skittish riptides. Though the beams spotlighting down from glass windows onto our islands are cool and silvery today, they needle hot into my skull and prick out sweat like acid rain on my skin. Gravity's pull seems to drag me down, down, and I hear an odd buzzing sound as I fight to stay conscious, stay on the chair, ride the breakers of ferocious pain and nausea and panic. Jesus! My body is a machine after all, and I'm losing control.

More sunshine. My eyes smart as I come to. The fiery pain, however, has been doused and the all-pervasive dark nausea has gone. I didn't realise I was carrying a set of heavy weights, but I was, and my mind and limbs no longer feel leaden. A grey fog has settled around me, but as light hits my eyes, images are focused again. A shadowy figure draws the curtains a little to shield my face, and the temperature instantly seems to drop. I sigh and sink back into pillows and into a mattress that moulds to my body even more efficiently than my chair at work. Work! My eyelids flicker in time to the runaway pulse of panic as I make a great effort to rise above some lingering wisps of fog. I'm not at work, and I'm not at home. Someone has beaten me up, or so it feels, and yet I feel better than I have in many weeks. I didn't realise how distanced I had become from my body, how much my appetite had waned, and suddenly I feel hungry again. In fact, I'm hollow as a barrel.

I move gingerly, and find I really am sore. I'm oddly bulky, too, padded up in a sort of nappy as if I have a heavy period. Knowledge knocks a little louder on my skull to be let out not in. Then, just as dreamlike, the door to the room opens and closes quietly, only to open and click closed again. A white-coated female takes a seat on the bed. But if I'm not at work... my brain moves at last into first gear. Ah:

either I am dreaming, or I'm in hospital. Simple! And if in hospital, then this brisk little person is a doctor. No sooner do I have the thought, than she is indeed introducing herself in a gravelly voice as Frau Doktor Claudia Dickbertel-Bopp. What a totally ridiculous name! Laughter froths gaily in my throat and I smile. I must be dreaming after all: sometimes my dreams are startlingly real.

Yet, as she talks, her words solidify. They're very real. They rasp against the air, sandpapering my nerves. I don't suppose she means to be accusing, but her tone is incredulous and hints strongly at blame as she informs and interrogates in equal measure. *Wie kann es sein...* how can it be that I, an intelligent person, didn't realise I was pregnant? Her voice, like nails on a blackboard, scrapes on about something called 'Rhesus Incompatibility'. Why did I not go to a doctor if I felt so ill? Hmm? Was I ever pregnant before? Why had there been no blood tests when I lost that first baby? It was the same father back then? Ah... then both babies inherited their blood group from their father (Yin)... not mine (Yang). Positive and negative are incompatible: the two eternal principles, contrary to myth, do not fit. My body, it seems, has been fighting my own child for survival.

Doktor Dickbertel-Bopp gets more corporeal by the second. She tries (and fails) to couch it all in acceptable terms. I don't have the energy to tell her I am an intelligent person after all and I've got the message: put simply, one of us had to go – if I'm alive, my child is dead. I have to face it finally: another child is dead. She rattles on. An extreme case: not usually as bad as this. Despite my... er... lack of awareness (she means stupidity), nothing I did or didn't do caused it. She's very, very sorry. She sighs. What is very sad is there could have been a chance, if the doctors had been more alert and the right action had been taken when the first pregnancy ended. After that little twist of the scalpel, she finishes off like a kind but stern headmistress: there should be no more pregnancies – I must understand that. A third time could be fatal.

That's another myth shattered, then: a third time, I might not be so lucky.

Hours later, I wake again and Micha is hunched miserably by the bed. He is haggard in the sick-white hospital light. I can see how blunted and ugly his bones are and what he will look like as an old man. When he sees I'm awake, his features lighten; his blue eyes sparkle. The lines etched deep between his brows disappear. I wince as he grabs my hand so hard it hurts. I struggle to understand what he's babbling about. Something about… It's so good to have me back again: God, he's been so miserable, so worried! It's all been like a bad dream. As if I wasn't there. As if I'd left him. He couldn't work out what was wrong – no one could work out what was wrong. I wasn't myself, but everything will be just fine now. Everything will be exactly as it once was. We can go back to normal.

I feel absolutely nothing at all, but I nod and try to smile. I notice he's taken the trouble to pick and bring a great bunch of yellow wildflowers and grasses from the woods near where we live, the woods I love so much. They're in water, but of course they're dead already: delicate and innocent victims of an impractically romantic gesture. But I'm well brought up, and I open my mouth to thank him. As I do, he startles me by leaning over and kissing me with some passion. There's no time to move away, and I go cold with distaste. How crass! How… disrespectful! I would like very much to hit him, but I can't. It feels as if we should both cry, but we don't. A part of my mind detaches from the scene, thinking of how it will help to dry those flowers and keep them in a box. Yes: that's what I'll do – then, wherever I go, just like Mad Queen Juana of Castile when she lost her weak but adored husband, I can keep them with me. She dragged her husband all over Europe in his coffin: my clinging and mourning will be more discreet.

Because Micha seems happy to witter on, I can be alone with my thoughts. His lips move, but I hear no sound. He seems almost obscenely happy to me. Well, I know he never wanted children as I did. Though another observer might be touched by his devotion and think he's taking it rather well, a cynic might conclude he's a mightily relieved man, for more reasons than one. Someone who judges others harshly might go so far as to think him a little heartless. I know the truth, but I also know that, within his limits, he is at least genuinely loving and honest. From now on, however, I will sit in a cold lonely halo of light putting words, gestures and feelings into patterns I've learned by heart. If I concentrate and do it all just right, I can make the machine work, even though I have no real understanding of what I'm doing and why.

Have you noticed that now machines are so absolutely integral to our lives, we're just not conscious of them when they're getting on with their jobs? We only remember them and what they do when the noise stops, in that awful moment when a machine shudders and dies into a shocked stillness. Even then, I suppose, the monotomy can be a kind of relief: at least you know the worst, and can usually get on with repairing it or replacing it with new. If you can't do that, though, you'll try desperately to deceive yourself that there's nothing wrong. You'll shut your mind and eyes and ears and pray to a god you don't believe in that it will keep going. Unwittingly, the machine can collude by teasing you and by going on relentlessly, even maddeningly – until, intelligent being or not, you're tantalised into believing your own idiotic untruth.

So who's really in control, do you think? I don't know the answer, by the way – I throw out the question in case anyone does. I do think machines have great advantages over us humans. I think it's most wonderful that, despite its built-in memory chip, a machine actually lives in an empty perpetual present. It can't think or feel pain or remember and – most comfortingly of all – it has no independence or ability to create and therefore no free will or decisions to make. A machine has no choices because it needs none. That's it. So simple: a machine works or it doesn't, and it's up to its masters and slaves to take action while it just chugs along blankly, appearing to conform to whatever its creator dictates. That's what happens, I guess, when someone takes out their memory chip and throws it away.

The Last of the Nest-Gatherers
Sascha Akhtar

I see them, the balinsasayaw, their swept back wings,
boomerangs gliding through the sky. Pappo says if I am
patient, I will yet witness their special aerial dances.

"They mate during the Monsoons, Kevin," Pappo tells me.
I await the rain.

I would accompany Pappo across the waters of the Sulu
Sea when he went off to work on the smaller islands of
Pabellon, with their brilliant white sands. We set off from
the port of TayTay. I was keen to learn our craft; the way
of the busyadores. To me, Pappo was Spiderman, scaling
the expanses of the limestone cliffs. I watched, breathless.
I believed him to have small, intricate mechanisms shoot
out sticky webs from his ankles. How else could he and
Grandpappo adhere to the slippery cave walls, towering
menacingly towards the sky? They had been climbing the karst
islands their whole lives, the tower-karsts, lovingly collecting
the nests of the birds. And the labyrinth of caves, where the
balinsasayaw nested were dark, glistening – hundreds of feet
high. Only those imbued with superpowers could do the
work they did.

I certainly knew the balinsasayaw had special powers, soaring,
as they did, high into the caves, spinning nests that clung
to the walls in a crescent shape, out of nothing, using only
their tiny-beaked mouths and their saliva. Grandmammo
narrated stories about the powers of the birds, to my sister
and I. Centuries ago, the balinsasayaw made nests just like the

other birds – in trees with twigs, grass, found bits – but they always struggled, their legs and feet out of proportion to their bodies.

"The balinsasayaw has big wing! Big, big and long wing! They love to fly, only fly. Walk— no."

I wondered what it must be like to live only in the sky.

"They were no good at making the nests! Their eggs not survive. The babies would lost! So they pray to Bird Goddess. 'Help Us!' They would chirp and chirrup, 'Help Us!'"

For ninety-two days and ninety-two nights, they prayed, Grandmammo narrated, until Bird Goddess descended from the clouds in half-human and half-bird form, a feather from every bird in the universe festooning her. Bird Goddess' eyes pierced, keener than those of eagles – orbs of swirling colours flickering in the centres. Her fine beak cast a grand shadow.

"What did she say Grandmammo? What did she say?" my younger sister squealed.

"She said in the strangest bird voice that only bird understand: 'I will help you. From now on your nests will be made... with only your mouth! You have been given the power to weave using the air and the water from your own cheeks. Your nests will be the strongest nests of all the birds and will stick on their own to the walls of your beloved caves. You will not have to try to build in the trees anymore.'"

"The balinsasayaw were very happy. They preferred the dark anyway. They sang all the melodies of the world in gratitude, honouring Bird Goddess."

"'There is something else— little balinsasayaw,' Bird Goddess continued. They stopped their songs to listen. 'The universe is made of balances. If I give you these powers to nurture your young, there is a price.'"

"The Queen balinsasayaw said, 'Your Most Excellent Bird Goddess, we worship you. You are our saviour, we are prepared.'"

"'The humans will want your nests. They are greedy and full of self-doubt and fear. You will have to forgive them. There is nothing that can be done to change them. They want to live forever. They are… ignorant…'"

"'Our nests?' The balinsasayaw were alarmed. 'But why?'"

"'Your nests will contain healing powers, unrivalled.' Bird Goddess told the birds that they would be able to raise their babies in their nests, but after that the humans would come for them!" Grandmammo gesticulated, her fingers slightly bent and knobbly in parts.

I knew the story. I knew all the stories; how for centuries the men in my family had sustained their families through gathering the coveted nests, selling them to the rich. The craggy, limestone cliffs, weathered into caverns and hollows of the remote archipelago of Pabellon had given my family everything. My father, grandfather and uncles traversed the aquamarine sea in engine-propelled bangkas fitted with bamboo outriggers, like they had done for generations.

We, my family and my village, continued the ancient ways of gathering nests, with nothing more than bamboo poles (which our village was famous for carving) and bundles of the finest bamboo rope made by my mother and women from other families. We sold these ropes to other nest-gatherers; busyadores.

"Your Mamma, she make the best rope. With her love."

My mother would smile when my father praised her so – before yelling at him. "I must to make the strongest ropes! You know how you tell a good bamboo rope from a bad one? If it sound hollow like cardboard it no good! Mine, not sound like cardboard, every year, new rope— new rope. Only Bamboo! No Rattan! I don't want you to die! When will you stop doing this work? You are crazy man!"

My father would, of course, laugh. "Crazy man! What crazy man! Crazy man make money for us! Money send Kevin and Elena to school!"

They would argue like this for a while. And this was the problem. My mother and grandmother feared for the men's lives constantly. My mother was reluctant to let me go with Pappo when I began to show an interest. She did not want this life for me.

It was true. We went to a very good school thanks to the balinsasayaw. Nobody in our family had ever gone to school. My grandmother complained that we spoke too much English and no longer understood our mother tongue, but Pappo was proud of that, which was why he always tried to speak to us in English – even though he wasn't sure of himself in it.

"Kevin— look, look." Pappo gestures excitedly, drawing my name out to sound like *Keveen*. It is time. The dance in mid-air has begun. The monsoons have finally arrived. I immediately spot the female; she has her wings unfurled. The male lands on her back and they plummet hundreds of feet towards the earth – gliding like unguided kites tangled up in a war. Their plumage fluttering in the accelerating winds, regardless they remain tightly intertwined. I am nervous that they will hurt themselves, not come apart in time and drown or get impaled on a jagged cliff face – so toothy and unforgiving.

They were as graceful in coming apart as they were in coming together. One bird drifted off on the air – East; the other, West. This was not goodbye, though. I knew what happened next. The Daddy bird was now in charge of creating the sacred nest. His salivary glands would swell as if by magic (well, I knew it was) when the time drew near for the eggs to be laid. Pappo says the Balinsasayaw have no choice. If they don't work on it daily, once the mating process has begun, their glands will get inflamed.

"It takes 35 days to build the nest! Poor bird!"

Uncle Jo has died. Those karsts are slippery. All the nest-gatherers, our community of busyadore, continue to gather nests, knowing full well the dangers of the caves. One wrong step is all it took. Most of them continued to climb barefoot – Grandpappo swore by it.

"You can feel the rock under your foot. You can sense its strength better," he liked to remind any busyadores with new-fangled ideas. When I would see Pappo and Uncle and Grandpappo moving along the walls like Spiderman, it also looked like a dance, but a slow one. Pappo always said to never ever remove hands unless certain of the rock beneath the feet. Some rocks were loose. But Uncle Jo had moved his hand. Something Pappo could never come to terms with.

I had witnessed first-hand the terrible death of Uncle Jo, but the story was being narrated over and over. He had removed his hand and the rock under his foot gave way. There was not a moment for anyone to save him.

When these accidents occurred, I often heard the adults say "It was his time". To be a busyadore was to have a nest-gathering clock on your back, and if the cave spirits so wished, their time could end. Some men managed to grow old before their busyadore clock ran out and were unable to continue climbing naturally – those were the lucky ones. And some like Uncle Jo, well, his clock had been set too early.

Stories were told, in hushed tones, of one gatherer who misjudged the tides and got stuck inside a cave for thirty-two days. Even in the darkness he survived by eating the bird's nest and the insects that eat the bird and bat dung off of the floor of the caves.

Eventually Grandmammo gave up telling Grandpappo to stop. She had tried everything, telling him about why it was a cursed job, how nothing good could ever come of stealing the most precious possession of the birds.

"Why you want to feed those rich, rich Manila people, China people, Vietnam people? Ah? Why? They so greedy, they want more and more all the time. How much they pay!! Thousand of dollar, thousand of dollar! For spit! For bird spit!" And she was right, of course, it was just bird spit after all.

None of us had ever experienced the coveted finery of bird's nest soup, served on the grandest of tables. But Grandpappo had been bringing bits home over the years.

I knew all the gradings of nest. Once, Pappo pulled out a specimen he was particularly proud of to show me.

"This is the most beautiful!" It sparkled and gleamed in the light – its delicate hairsbreadth strands of saliva hardened. I imagined the little swiftlet in a frenzy, flying back and forth and around and around – an aerial weaver making a miniature canoe, with peaks on either end, deep and roomy in the centre to support the eggs and then the babies. The bottom was sturdy. Its form echoed my father's bangka. I had been very young then and reached forward with clumsy gait for it.

"Pappo! I want to play with the boat!" I said. Pappo laughed his head off.

"This? You want to play with this! This the most expensive food eaten by people in the whole world!"

It was. To this day it is. About 2500 U.S. dollars per kilogram for the best ones – like the one I had wanted to play with. The most intact and the cleanest (cleaned by our hands, of dirt and feathers using a blade) were the "A" grade – the lesser nests were "B" and "C". Grandpappo's 'ungraded', debris also brought in money, for not even the slightest filament of nest was without a price.

Grandpappo heard about the nests' healing powers (and he knew about the tale of Bird Goddess). He told me about all the minerals in the nest. Grandmammo's arthritis made it hard for her to work, so he had been secretly feeding her bits he managed to save. When she found out, she refused to take another bite.

Her arthritis flared up. Her aches and pains returned.

"Eh Bulanon. C'mon. You know it will help you." Grandpappo coaxed using his pet name for her (meaning crazy moon person). My sister and I worked on her as well, and from our hands, she begrudgingly gulped down some bird's nest.

Within a few days, her face appeared less tired and her complexion was light and pain-free, almost as if growing younger. My sister and I whispered. Bird Goddess really had imbued those nests with special medicine. Grandpappo was happy she was better, even though she would not admit it. He watched her doing her chores again without much discomfort. But still, he was worried.

"What is it Grandpappo? Aren't you happy? It worked! She is taking the medicine."

"Aye she is, but Kevin— I do not know how much longer I will be able to *bring* her the medicine."

"Why Grandpappo?" I thought he was talking of the cost, and immediately vowed if that was the case, I would help figure it out. I would become rich. I would buy her the nests.

"You will buy her the nests!" He roared with laughter, then grew solemn again. "Oh, my son— it is not that. I am afraid our days are numbered. We may be the last of the nest-gatherers."

"But Grandpappo— you always talk about the family tradition!" He loved telling me how just as he and I were three generations of one family, so too had he tended to generations of the same family of birds. "What about the balinsasayaw families? Are they not under our care?"

But Grandpappo did not reply. I wondered if this might be a good time to divulge the secret I'd been dreading telling him and Pappo.

My mother already knew. I did not want to join our family to become a busyadore. Mammo was right; it was a dangerous occupation and I wanted to be like her instead. She helped people in the village get better. I wanted to be a doctor and teach those who thought bird's nests were the only way, how to be well. I would heal people like Grandmammo. If people stopped bothering the balinsasayaw, they too would be protected.

Perhaps I could reverse Bird Goddess' prophecy.

But his face was a map of sadness. I decided not to tell him.

In December, I was allowed to go with Pappo for the onset of the next season. We sailed in groups of about a dozen unwieldy bangkas.

Early nest-gatherers had used tree sap wrapped in palm leaves to light their way through the karsts. We had torches now. I really liked the hats with lights on them, like miners underground.

The boats contained those and our other necessary tools, stacks and bundles of hard and soft implements, almost exclusively crafted from the bamboo.

It took about an hour to get to the smaller islands from the main island of Palawan, the most beautiful island in the world, it was called. Once we arrived it would be all go go go, so I sat back and watched the patterns the water made as we cut through it with our powered canoes. The waves in motion looked like a giant-tailed merman following us, the outline of the fin shape just visible beneath the water.

Pappo chatted – they wondered what the harvest would be like this year. They discussed the various storms we had experienced and whether they may have affected the bird's breeding patterns. Pappo was excited to see his caves again. He loved the birds as much as he loved us, as did Grandpappo. They had both been the guardians of the same caves as far back as they could remember.

"We have been tasked with a sacred honour," Grandpappo was solemn. Every family was responsible for a specific cave system, and for ensuring the protection of the species. "These new gatherers! They stress the balinsasayaw! They don't wait for them to raise their babies!"

Grandpappo could not bear any ill treatment of the birds or their precious nests. I saw how they consulted him with the changing seasons, and when he spoke a hush washed over the land, as all strained in to listen. Above all, he waited for the birds to complete their cycle, never throwing eggs out of the nest to speed up the process. The floors of the caves under his protection would never be littered with broken eggshells. They were renowned for their prosperous harvest. The birds came back year after year, as if in a pact with him.

As we got closer to the rocky shores, Grandpappo clapped his hands together. "Limpiada!" he shouted. "Are we ready for limpiada?"

All of us cheered.

"In order to begin, Kevin," Pappo explained, "we must first clean their caves. Limpiada!"

"Clean? Why?" They were just birds. It didn't make sense.

"The birds will not make their nests, if we not to clean the walls! If we didn't clean every year, the birds would not come back! We remove old guano. We scrub the walls. We look after them. We don't disturb them. We wait until they let us come."

Once we reached the island, we unloaded. That took ages! There were the poles and special knives, three-pronged tweezers blessed by the cave spirits to cut and pull the nests off the cave walls and ropes and sticks which had bent forks at the end – used when the nest was hard to approach. Like play forts, small huts were dotted amongst the large rocks all along the coast, from previous seasons for us to clean in, rest or eat. I would sit in them and pretend to be the captain of a mighty ship, like the great Chinese fleet admiral Zheng He, sailing in the 15th Century...

Every bird's nest-gathering family knew how the bird's nest was discovered. The formidable Chinese admiral was travelling the Western Seas when the chaos of a storm tossed him to a Malay-side desert island.

I was the admiral ordering my crew to stay calm. I steered the ship to safety from the threatening winds and waters rising in the vessel. We ran aground hoping to shelter from the storm, but soon we were low on food.

"The supplies are dwindling, Admiral. The men are getting weak."

"Have we been able to locate fresh water?"

"Yes, Admiral, there are rock pools amongst the caves over yonder."

"And what of the vegetation? The flora? The fauna?"

"We are trying other sides of the island, but the fishing is not as we would hope."

Admiral Zheng He stared out at the ocean. He was not sure when they would be able to set off again, and he had a thirty-strong crew. The oracles had not warned him of this storm. The stars had betrayed him! And they had given him a puzzling message: *You will set off a cycle of events that will unfurl for centuries and will lead to the End times. Be careful of the choices you make in the course of your protection.*

It was clear now to Admiral Zheng He that the storm was part of this puzzle – but what was it the oracles had seen? He must choose carefully? But what was it he must choose?

"Caves you say?"

"Yes Admiral."

"Investigate the caves. We may have to eat bats, Huang. It is now a matter of our survival. We must return to the Emperor with the sacred scrolls— and for that we need to stay alive. Have every man scouring the rocks and the caves."

"As you wish, Admiral."

The men had come back after a day – bruised and bloodied, holding strange, translucent objects like tiny canoes. The sun was not strong on the island that day. Clouds clustered in the sky, obscuring the light. The objects the men held glimmered like mother-of-pearl. Admiral Zheng He examined them. He had not seen anything resembling their delicate forms. The men relayed that they found them like that, empty, but adhering to the steep rock walls inside the caves.

Huang was almost certain they were bird's nests, as there were feathers and egg shells in them. *Be careful of the choices you make in the course of your protection*, the prophecy had cautioned.

The men were lean and hungry. With difficulty, the Admiral broke off a few strands of the nest and put them in his mouth, the texture chewy like raw noodles. He stayed in thought a while. Perhaps they would behave as noodles did and provide a hearty soup for the starving men.

"Huang, I want you to boil these nests in water," Huang, the Admiral's right-hand also acted as the chef of the ship. Fortunately, they had retained a scattering of ingredients with them – ginseng, dried mushroom, five-spice. Those would serve well for soup.

I had learnt about the Admiral in school. A few days of drinking the soup and his whole crew were revived. He believed he had been led to it by the Celestial Beings. He brought this magical healing object to the Emperor Ming Cheng Zu and his name was remembered forever.

I, too, never forgot the story. I wanted to know how these bird's nests had such strong healing properties. When Grandmammo she started taking it, I was amazed at the change. Once I was a doctor, I would be able to learn all about these things. But the message of the stars that the Admiral received perplexed me. Had he made the wrong choice to take from the balinsasayaw? I didn't like the sound of the 'End Times'.

I disappeared into the hut almost as soon as we arrived. I knew it would take about an hour of setting up the ropes and ladders of bamboo before the busyadores were ready to start the cleaning work, let alone begin gathering. I was lost to the world of Admiral Zheng He, not knowing that day everything was to change.

Then, sharp, explosive sounds erupted outside the hut. Machine guns? But it couldn't be. Men were shouting, my father calling my name, then others, too. What should I do? I didn't dare step out from the entrance of the hut, but I peeked around. My father! I couldn't make out what was happening, everyone was running towards the shore, towards the boats.

"Kev-O! Come! Come!" My father raced towards the hut, I towards him.

"What's happening Pappo?"

"No time, no time!" He grabbed my hand, heading

towards the bangkas. It was madness. I looked for Grandpappo but couldn't see him.

Pappo was frantic. The repetitive action of his arm, willed the motor into action. Indistinct figures dotted all along the cliff tops. People I'd never seen. Me, crouching down in the boat. Ocean spray hitting Pappo's face as the vessel hit the water. Bursts of assault rifle rounds shooting into the skies. Just before the cliffs became obscured from sight, I saw them. The balinsasayaw falling swiftly, dead from the skies.

The bird moves its head back and forth like a weaving bobbin. The bird starts by flying persistently in front of its chosen site and repeatedly dabbing the rock with its tongue, laying down a curved line of saliva, which marks the lower edge of the nest-to-be. The saliva dries and hardens quickly and with repeated flights, the bird slowly builds up the low line into a low wall. As soon as this is big enough to cling to, the speed of the construction accelerates. Within a few days, the wall becomes a semi-circular cup of creamy white interlacing string just big enough to hold the customary clutch of two eggs[1].

Legend had it that the imperial emperors and empresses coveted one nest above all – a nest of deep reddish-brown colour. The blood nest. The balinsasayaw needed to shed blood from inside its mouth to weave. The Empress demanded only those. Over the centuries, the blood nest acquired a mythical status. Scientists carried out research and debunked the blood theory.

"There is no blood," they said.

"Specific minerals leach into the nests from cave walls," they said.

1   *Sir David Attenborough quoted in journal Facts and Details South-East Asia on the Swiftlet; Jeffrey Hays 2008.*

But the old nest-gatherers knew: when the birds were stressed, they bled. Poachers and uncaring gatherers under pressure from violent, ruthless bosses would steal the nests and hurl the eggs onto the cave floors. Cruel pools of broken shell, albumen and precious DNA-containing yolk would spread – the Unborn birds. The balinsasayaw were already the fastest birds on earth. They had to speed up even more to protect their young, to ensure their continued existence, to build the nests faster and higher on the cave walls. And so they would bleed.

The world's wealthiest woman sits on an iridescent glass throne in a penthouse apartment aglow with sunlight atop Hong Kong's highest point, Mount Nicholson, 1,411 feet above the city. In the midst of a world of glass, she is positioned, ghost-like, at a table. Before her, steam rises up from a fine porcelain bowl inlaid with gold filigree, obscuring her face. She reaches fluidly to her right, as if performing the first movement of a dance for the curved arm of a porcelain soup spoon. She takes a deep breath in and out, moving the spoon precisely towards the bowl's centre, into the depths of the pearly, gelatinous liquid.

A bloody-looking thing is unravelling, like a ball of string. Thinly-knifed pale green and white slices of spring onion float on atop, some still interlinked; miniature islands

The spoon reaches her lips, parting to receive the liquid. Red strands hang over the curve of her bottom lip, which she moves into the cavity of her mouth, with a flick of the tongue, as she has done for centuries.

The lift lights up as it reaches the 111th floor. The glass doors slide open silently as two black-clad hulking figures stride in.

"Empress. It is done. We have secured the last of the islands from those fool nest-gatherers." The taller of the two laughs with particular glee.

"Every island of caves through Malaysia, the Philippines and Borneo now have our men positioned with assault rifles, and if any of them try to enter we shoot and throw them into the ocean," added the other one.

The Empress gleams – surrounded as she is by a kaleidoscope of reflections and light, but there is something else – an otherworldly quality come from having gained immortality. Her skin is iridescent like the saliva of the swiftlets when it hardens into nest.

"And the Governments? Our agreements are in place?"

"Yes, your Imperial Majesty, we control the market now. And we will ensure that the balinsasayaw *remain* stressed."

The Empress said nothing, continuing to polish off her blood nest soup.

"Bird Goddess, O Bird Goddess, we beseech you. Please come to us. We can no longer survive. It was just as you said. The humans! They are greedy, so greedy. It was just as you said."

The winds travelled swiftly over the ocean, like a horse galloping. The ground rumbled. A song began, so glorious that the birds felt their spirits soar. Bird Goddess appeared exactly as she had at the beginning of time.

"Balinsasayaw! I come to you now. What is it that you want? I did what you asked me, but over the humans— I have no power."

"Bird Goddess. We cannot keep up. They kill our babies, but they want us to keep making nests and keep making nests woven with our blood. Our blood! We want this to end."

"End? How?"

"We are ready to leave, Bird Goddess. We want to leave this world. Like so many of our species before us who chose to leave the humans. We cannot help them anymore. We cannot tend to the Earth."

"I told you, you would have to forgive them."

"We forgive them! We forgive them! But we must leave now. They are blood-thirsty. This is no place for us and many others in time, too, shall follow. We must leave Earth."

"Very well, little balinsasayaw. You have always had a choice, and I honour how long you have kept the Sacred Covenant to look over the humans and the Earth."

"It shall be done."

Pappo and I were fortunate to have our lives. We learnt about the mafia take-over of the bird's nest-gathering work. It was what Grandpappo had been hinting at to me. He had known what was coming.

Many of the villagers had not made it back. We were a village in mourning for too many months. Poor Grandpappo nearly lost his leg, were it not for Mammo's healing powers. He had just made it out on the last boat, helping as many injured off the islands as he could.

"They shot me!" he roared, emitting a string of expletives we were not allowed to repeat. But we prayed and gave thanks every day that he had survived.

Then one day Pappo came running home, shouting and yelling.

"They are gone! They are gone!"

"Who is gone? What are you talking about?" Grandpappo yelled.

"The balinsasayaw, everyone is talking about it. The news. The radio. The newspapers."

Grandmammo stood in the doorway, listening. My sister and I did not understand what Pappo could mean. How could they be gone? They were birds! Birds did not just disappear.

Crowded around the television at Jim's house, we watched alarmed newscasters relay the story. A news team even came to our village to interview one of us! The mating season had begun, but not one bird was seen from across Malaysia, Thailand or the Philippines. The nest-gatherers, the buyers, the luxury restaurants, everyone waited and waited.

But the balinsasayaw never appeared.

"Empress! Empress! Where are you?" A barrel-chested male army swarmed through the penthouse, having searched everywhere. Her blood nest supply had been dwindling. She had been forced to draw on reserve supplies to keep her going, changing in hue and texture. Veins now appeared to pulse under the surface of her skin, developing crags and folds.

The Empress made no movement without their knowledge and protection. Her disappearance led them to only one conclusion; she had been kidnapped.

"Empress!" The men believed they would locate her. Frantic calls were made all over the globe. The Empress' network was exhaustive and far-reaching. Her power, absolute. Had they not been in such a panic, they might have noticed the Empress' fine Qing Dynasty bowl still lay on the frosted glass surface of the table. It was only ever out when she was having her soup. They might have noticed further the steam rising from it, just as if the Empress was seated right there, engaged in her ritual.

Were they to look closer, they would see that the spoon next to the bowl was oddly coated, that a thick, liquid oozed down the intricate carvings of swiftlets on the back of the glass throne, behind the bowl. A viscous liquid, streaked with long, thickened, streams of rust-coloured blood, pooled onto the pristine white statuario marble floor.

In the centre of the bowl, the usual ball of yarn, the nest of the balinsasayaw, vanished, leaving circles of spring onion islands floating alone in a blood-fragrant bisque.

Pass Through the Waters
Kenzie Millar

My Dearest Elizabeth,

I must once again profess my gratitude to you in procuring such an ideal situation as Reed Cottage for Mary and myself.

Mr Thomson could not have found a more pleasing place for us, on all his properties. It is exactly right for us and should only need the assistance of a girl to come each day. Which, as you know, is all my current income will allow.

I find I am blessed with such kind relations, as Mr Thomson and yourself not only took us in after my poor William passed away, but now have found somewhere my child and I can grow to be happy, despite our losses.

I know you will not have seen Reed Cottage yourself, having not travelled to this area of the country, so I have included a small sketch of the lovely house and garden. Note, the trailing honeysuckle, which you will remember is a favourite of mine.

I will, of course, write to you soon, and tell you how the neighbourhood is. I simply had to write to you now to inform you that we are arrived safely.

Yours, in eternal gratitude,

Cass

Reed Cottage did not have honeysuckle growing in the garden. The house faced out on too wild a prospect for such delicate plants. But she wanted her sister to think her happy. Elizabeth had pleaded with Cass to stay with her and her husband George, and their boys. Cass couldn't bear to, though. Just four years as mistress of her own home had given her a taste of independence she could not give up, not along with losing poor William. Poor, poor William. A naval officer with a ready smile and good prospects for his future. A hard worker, his optimism had balanced Cass's propensity to worry and melancholy. And then the sea had taken him from her and their daughter, the waves laughing at all his plans.

"You are lucky," her brother-in-law had said, unfolding his newspaper, "that he put aside money and invested. I'll happily pay my man to manage it for you and you shall be comfortable. You will even have enough for a small dowry for Mary. Not many widows have such luck. Of course, if you were to marry again, you would find life a lot easier…"

"It is too soon to talk of that," Elizabeth said. "Cassie will marry again, once her grief has passed." She said this with the certain knowledge of an older sister. "You would not wish me to think of marrying again so soon, if you were to die."

"No, I suppose not. Though it is different, of course. We have the boys and they would be able to look after you."

"And Cassie and Mary have us."

Lucky, so very lucky, to find someone who occasionally seemed to understand her, then for that to be taken away. No, she would not find someone else she wished to marry. No one else she would risk her happiness for again.

Although it was by no means what she and Elizabeth had been used to, either growing up or in marriage, Reed Cottage did have some charm. From the rocky garden, Cass could sit and watch the sea. Elizabeth had worried she would grieve more looking at the very thing that had taken poor William, but she didn't. She loved to watch the chaotic nature of something impossible for man to harness. They might fool themselves that they had dominion over the sea, with their ships and their Empire, but that would never truly be the case.

Cass sat on an old chair. Mary toddled around, pulling weeds and presenting them to her like orchids. Cass hugged a shawl close around her. The wind was biting and rain could appear at any time. She watched the cove below as the sea stole pebbles and sand, beating itself against the rocks.

The sun dipped towards the horizon. Orange rays reflected in the grey mirror of waves. She should put Mary to bed. Cass had to be up early. And yet, she couldn't raise herself. Just a few weeks of living here and she couldn't imagine not getting to see this sight each evening. Even if it rained, the sunset obscured by grey clouds, she stood in the arch of the doorway, feeling the change as day turned to night.

"This is a magical hour, little Bean," Cass said, her voice soft so as not to disturb the emptiness. "A time for fairies and sprites to appear. You must always watch out for them as not all are good."

Despite exhaustion weighing her eyelids, and the comfortable bed, she could not sleep. Cass's mind would not calm. Eventually, she took her shawl and a lantern and walked towards the beach. Perhaps the night air and the sound of waves would soothe her. No particular worry kept her from sleep. Mary was well. They were settling into their new life, and she finally had space to breathe, perhaps for the first time since poor William had died. Maybe grief kept her mind from stilling. But she didn't feel sad.

The lantern cast a cold orb of light around her, the world beyond mere ghostly shapes. At the beach, she placed it carefully on the sand, and left her slippers and stockings next to it. She continued without its blinding light, letting her eyes adjust and her feet feel the sand. What would Elizabeth think of her, wandering alone at night, stockingless. Only a certain type of woman would do such a thing.

She spread her arms, let the shawl whip behind her. The almost full moon cast the beach with silver. The colour had disappeared from the world. And then she saw her.

18th July

She sat on the rocks, studying the movements of a rock pool. Her skin was so pale it reflected the moonlight. I knew then, she had stopped me sleeping. Thoughts of her creamy skin, naked to the air. Though I had my shawl wrapped around me, I felt my skin goosepimple, just looking at her.

I never had the courage to approach her until last night. I knew I wouldn't be able to sleep until I spoke to her. Twice before I had seen her, but just from the garden. I wasn't even sure she wasn't some dream. I made myself step forward.

"Hello, I... are you alright?"

Her eyes glinted. I am not sure what colour they are, in the moonlight they looked grey.

"Hello." Her voice was... almost musical. It had a rhythm I did not recognise as the local accent, though neither anything like my own clipped tones.

"Where have you come from?"

It felt rude, brusque. And yet what etiquette was there to talking to a naked woman at night?

"The sea," she said, simply.

"You come from the sea?"

"I do." Her lips curled into a smile, parting slightly to show white teeth. "Where do you come from?"

"I live in Reed Cottage."

"I do not know it."

I gestured behind me. "It's up there." How anyone could be here on this beach and not know the house was beyond me. It was then I saw the skin. I had mistaken it for a rock, dark, almost black and glistening with sea water. As I looked now, I saw fur – a seal skin. And then I knew what she was, this creature in front of me. She could only be a selkie. A creature part seal, part woman, that my nursemaid had told me of on dark winter nights. Could she be real?

My Dearest Elizabeth,

This is a great place for Mary to grow, for us both to recover from our loss. There is something about the vastness of the sea, of its constant changing. It puts everything into perspective. What must God know of my worries and ills, He who created the oceans and the lands for us to live on? As it is said in Psalms: "There is the sea, vast and spacious, teeming with creatures beyond number — living things both large and small." And through prayer, he comforts and aids me, just one of his many creatures. It is truly wondrous.

The Rector here preaches very nicely. I enjoy our visits to church, although I do find it difficult to keep little Mary still. I believe here I can really develop in my knowledge and love of the Lord, despite all He has laid before us.

Your beloved sister,

Cass

Her letters to Elizabeth grew shorter each week. For what could she tell her sensible sister of her life here? "My darling Elizabeth, our nursemaid's tales were true. There are women who change from seals. Perhaps fairies also dance around mushroom rings?" No, Elizabeth would have her committed to an Asylum with talk such as that.

Each night, regardless, she went to the beach and talked to Selena, for that was the creature, the woman's name. Selena told her about the world under the sea. How the sunlight turned all into greens, while the moon seemed to suck the colour out again. She asked about Cass. What her life was like.

"I lost my husband, William, last year. It's just me and my daughter now."

"You do not like being alone," Selena stated.

"No… I thought that I should prefer to live independently. But it is a quiet life, to have no one, not even to wait for their return. William was often away for a long time, but it does not feel the same."

The selkie reached her hand to Cass's cheek, brushed tears away with her thumb. Her hand was so soft, silken even.

"I wish you were not alone. We often live years on our own, though it is a joy to see our sisters."

"You have sisters?" Cass asked, sniffing.

"Oh, many, many sisters. We are all sisters under the sea."

"There are no… men?"

Selena shrugged. "There are some males, they are sisters too. We are all selkie."

"For humans, everything is different if you are born a man or a woman. It is men who get to travel the world, while we women are left at home."

"Strange." Selena looked out at the star-dipped night. "We do not really think of this thing you call a home. In the sea, change is eternal."

2nd August

My conversations with Selena stay with me, even as the daylight tries to make a dream of them. There is more for me to do here, more for my hands, but my mind is free to wander.

I think of what I want for my Mary. While I yearn for the changing world Selena describes, I know I was always given an anchor in my childhood. My steady mother and father, God rest their souls, may have lived a small life, but they were present. Mary has only me to anchor her. A woman with no substance at all.

"Come into the sea with me," Selena said one night, as they sat shoulder to shoulder on the sand. It was neither a question or a demand.

"I have no bathing dress."

A laugh. "Neither do I." She stood, skin silver in the moonlight. Cass couldn't help but look in awe of her beauty as Selena stood there, so comfortable in this body that wasn't even fully her own. Her hips and stomach were larger than Cass's, curved and cresting. Selena's long black hair moved constantly, though the night seemed still. It trailed over her full breasts, her dark nipples.

She smiled down at her, hand outstretched. "You will like it, I think."

Cass took her hand and allowed Selena to pull her to her feet. Before she could reach down herself, Selena bent to catch the bottom of her nightgown. Cass let the selkie pull the material up and over her body. She did not feel the night's chill, so focused was she on Selena's smiling face.

"I shall leave my skin here, and come into the sea like you."

Cass nodded. She took the selkie's hand, caressing it with her thumb. Warmth spread up her arm from where they touched, and she yearned to pull Selena closer. Together, they walked to the waves. The beach was sheltered so the sea here merely started as a cold tickle of her feet. They kept moving forward, Selena's hand giving her some courage.

Soon enough, the water reached Cass's breasts, her shoulders.

"Lift your feet. You can hold onto me."

And she did. She wrapped her arms around Selena, letting the selkie hold her up as the waves gently raised and lowered them. Cass knew she should feel scared, and yet she only felt secure in Selena's arms. The warmth she had felt from holding Selena's hand was pooled now in her stomach. Fluttering excitement, yet certainty too. This was where she was supposed to be.

"Cassie," Selena asked. "May I kiss you?"

"Yes," she whispered.

The selkie's lips tasted of the salt water all around them.

10th August

Selena wants to meet Mary. I am so scared, and yet I so want to see my daughter and Selena together. I believe Mary would love her. Just as I think I do.

The day was warm, a real summer day. Cass walked to the beach with Mary on her hip. Strange, to travel down this familiar path in the daylight. Her feet were confident and yet her eyes noticed things that were invisible in the dark – rocks, plants, spiky sea grass.

She had left one of her own dresses on the beach that morning, had warned Selena that Mary would find it too strange if she did not wear something familiar. But seeing Selena covered in green muslin still shocked her. The dress suited her, though it hid her intriguing curves and silky skin. And though it should have made her look more human, the dress couldn't hide that Selena's creamy skin glowed slightly. She still looked as if she was lit by moonlight. Her black hair still moved on its own. Not wildly, just a gentle stir one could miss. Cass though, could always see everything about Selena.

"This is Selena, Mary. She is a friend of Mamma."

Mary waved her hands in the air.

"Hello, Mary," Selena said, with her usual smile. "Hello, Cass."

"You look beautiful in that dress."

Selena laughed, and spun around so the skirt furled. "What strange devices you humans have. It seems so unnecessary. But it is pretty, I suppose."

Mary laughed and struggled to get down. With her feet on the sands, she twirled alongside Selena. Cass couldn't help it, she laughed too, seeing her daughter dancing with a selkie.

My Dearest Elizabeth,

I am so excited that it will soon be Christmas. Mary and I so look forward to visiting you and the boys at the Hall and telling you of all our adventures.

It is really a quiet life here, as I have said before, so I do not have too much to write about. Mary is happy growing by the sea, spending her days collecting little shells to give to me.

I have decided to hire a new woman to help me here at Reed Cottage. She is also a widow and we have found some comfort together. She is very kindly to Mary as her marriage was not blessed with children before her husband's death. She is happy to live here with us and help me with some of the work I am less familiar with, so that I may concentrate on instructing Mary and my own relationship with God.

Yours, ever,

Cass

20th November

Mere months since Selena entered my life, and yet I cannot imagine ever being without her. Nights are spent not on the beach, but in my bed. Our bed. Her kisses along my thighs still shock me with their tenderness.

She spends each morning with Mary in her room, singing strange songs that make Mary laugh in a way I have never heard before. Yesterday, I heard them from the kitchen.

"Where I come from, animals play with my sisters. The most amazing creatures."

"What animals?" Mary asked, her voice whispered excitement. She loved to meet animals and was especially fond of the cat she saw when we went to church.

"Oh many, things you haven't seen before. My favourite are seals. One day, we may see them from the beach. They love to swim and dance in the waves."

"I would like that, please."

The love my daughter has for Selena makes my feelings grow so fast it hurts. After William's death, I thought there would be Mary only. I thought of her growing up and away, leaving me alone once more. And yet now I see I have more than Mary, as Mary has more than me.

Selena spends less and less time returning to the sea. I feel scared to ask her about her life there. I fear that one day she will not return to us.

They stood together over William's old sea trunk. It had held some of his books, but Cass had taken these out. Perhaps she could sell them, one day, but for now they could be kept on one of the kitchen shelves. Unlike Selena's skin, which must stay hidden. Not that they had many visitors, especially now Cass had dismissed the servant girl. The Rector would still come to visit though, or for tea, and she did not want for him to have questions.

The dark fur was dry now, though it still seemed to glisten to Cass's eyes.

"Are you sure?" she asked again.

Selena smiled, widely. "I have always been happy to spend my time alone, just to find my way in the sea, until I met you Cass. This is not something you have asked of me, but something I wish to give you. Without my skin, I cannot return to my home or my sisters. I know that when the time comes, you will give me the skin and let me go. For that is what love is, is it not? The choice to remain together."

Selena shut the lid of the trunk. Cass felt those sparks deep in her stomach again, excitement. Selena had seen her fears. She didn't run from them. Cass knew she shouldn't run either. She felt warmth in her stomach as she chose. Chose Selena. Chose to remain.

"Cass, can I kiss you?"

"Yes, please."

Author Biographies

Gaynor Jones is the recipient of a Northern Writer's Award for her short story collection, Girls Who Get Taken.She has won first prize in several fiction competitions, including the Bath Flash Fiction Prize and the Mairtín Crawford Short Story Award, and has placed or been listed in others including the Bridport Prize and Aesthetica.

She has performed her work at many spoken word nights in the North, and as a guest of For Books' Sake at the 2019 Edinburgh Fringe. She loves stories that feature wayward teens, middle-aged women who've had enough, and the darker sides of suburban life.

Helen Nathaniel-Fulton originates from Swansea, but is now based in Paisley in Scotland. She studied History & History of Art at Aberystwyth University, Social Sciences at Oxford, & lived for many years in Kenya where she was a teacher with VSO. She's a retired children & families social worker who now paints & writes full-time. She has had a pamphlet of stories published called Da Vinci's Cuckoos & has been published in Scottish magazines Laldy! & Southlight & in the anthology Bridges or Walls? (Dove Tales, 2019).

Clayton Lister lives in Northumberland. His stories can be found here and there, but take care looking for them because they're shy and very easily frightened. Shhh...

Kenzie Millar is a writer, reviewer, and banker (well, she works for a bank at least). From her first book, written age 11, "Mustard Seeds", she knew she wanted to be an author and give her readers the magical gift of being taken to another world. While Kenzie-World has grown somewhat darker, she still hopes her readers will enjoy the discomfort and unease she creates. Her short stories are inspired by folk lore and fantasy, but focus on themes of motherhood, gender, and chronic pain. As you read, you should always question the story you are being told.

Kenzie was a runner up in the Orton 2020 competition, with her story Yuletide. Subsequently, she judged their 2021 competition. She has performed at The Other, Endostravaganza, and We Want Women. She is part of the Orton Writer's Group, and reviews books for the Crack magazine.

Sascha Akhtar is a maverick who writes, translates and teaches. Akhtar's course 'Breaking Through Writer's Block,' has been published by The Literary Consultancy, London as part of their ground-breaking #BeingAWriterprogramme. She is the author of six collections of poetry, and one fiction: Of Necessity And Wanting, published in 2020 has been shortlisted for the UBL Literary Award For Excellence in the Debut Fiction category.

Her shorter fictions appear in The Fortnightly Review, Queen Mobs Teahouse, Storgy BlazeVox, Tears In The Fence, The Learned Pig, Anti-Heroin Chic & MookyChick.

The Belles-Lettres of Hijab Imtiaz, a translated work of pioneering feminist fiction writer from the Indian Subcontinent is due in July 2022 with Oxford University Press, India. Akhtar is an advocate for community languages and has been working in schools with children as part of The Stephen Spender Trust's programme. She was a judge for the Stephen Spender Prize in 2021.

About Fly on the Wall Press

A publisher with a conscience.
Publishing high quality stories, poetry and anthologies on pressing issues, from exceptional writers around the globe.
Founded in 2018 by founding editor, Isabelle Kenyon.

A sample of other publications:

Bad Mommy / Stay Mommy by Elisabeth Horan
The Woman With An Owl Tattoo by Anne Walsh Donnelly
the sea refuses no river by Bethany Rivers
White Light White Peak by Simon Corble
Small Press Publishing: The Dos and Don'ts by Isabelle Kenyon
Grenade Genie by Tom McColl
House of Weeds by Amy Kean and Jack Wallington
No Home In This World by Kevin Crowe
The Goddess of Macau by Graeme Hall
The Prettyboys of Gangster Town by Martin Grey
The Sound of the Earth Singing to Herself by Ricky Ray
Inherent by Lucia Orellana Damacela
Medusa Retold by Sarah Wallis
Pigskin by David Hartley
We Are All Somebody
Someone Is Missing Me by Tina Tamsho-Thomas
Aftereffects by Jiye Lee
No One Has Any Intention of Building a Wall by Ruth Brandt
The House with Two Letter-Boxes by Janet H Swinney
The Guts of a Mackerel by Clare Reddaway
Snapshots of the Apocalypse by Katy Wimhurst

Social Media:
@fly_press (Twitter)
@flyonthewall_poetry (Instagram)
@flyonthewallpress (Facebook)
www.flyonthewallpress.co.uk